THE CASTLE ABDUCTIONS

Bailiff Mountsorrel Mysteries
Book One

David Field

SAPERE
BOOKS

THE CASTLE ABDUCTIONS

Published by Sapere Books.

24 Trafalgar Road, Ilkley, LS29 8HH,
United Kingdom

saperebooks.com

ISBN: 978-0-85495-205-2

1

Nottingham, 1590

Edward Mountsorrel crouched in the bracken of the deer park that was such a proud feature of the newly created Wollaton estate, four miles to the west of Nottingham. Behind him were the estate workers employed by the owner of the estate, Sir Francis Willoughby, and at the top of the hill, barely visible through the evening mist, was the magnificent Hall, completed two years previously in time to celebrate the glorious defeat of the Spanish Armada.

Edward had been a foot soldier then, part of the Leicestershire Trained Band that he had helped to march down to Tilbury to answer the call of Robert Dudley, Earl of Leicester. Dudley had rallied Elizabeth's ground troops to defend the Thames approaches to London, in case the navy under the command of Howard, Drake and Hawkins failed to stop the invaders at sea. Dudley had recognised something special in Edward — back then a twenty-five-year-old orphan turned soldier — and had recommended him for the post of bailiff to the High Sheriff of Nottinghamshire. It was in this capacity that he was now bent double on a late autumn evening, waiting to pounce on deer poachers.

The information he'd received was to the effect that a group of felons from the town were planning on driving a group of beasts down the side of the shallow natural lake behind the waiting men, and out through the narrow gate that led into Wollaton Vale. When they did so, they would be in for a very unpleasant surprise, and a collection of cracked skulls, when

Edward and Willoughby's men rose up from their hiding places and set about them with the heavy staffs with which they were armed.

The only sound came from the wildfowl that were bedding down for the night. Ahead of him, Edward could just make out the occasional group of grazing hinds with their young, jealously guarded by their stags. Other than that, there was nothing to see, and the mutterings of the estate men behind him indicated that they were becoming impatient. The thickening mist was cold and forbidding, and there were rumours that this area of the park was haunted by the wandering spirit of a former herdsman.

It was fully dark by the time Edward called a halt to the vigil with the unconvincing excuse that his source had probably been wrong about the day, and so the men would need to repeat their watch the following evening. The groans that this generated almost drowned out the distant shout from down near the Derby Road gate to their east, but Edward's trained ear picked it out. He ordered the men to follow him through the deer park towards it. Through the mist they could discern a man lying on the ground near the open gate, and as they got closer it became obvious that he'd been badly beaten.

'It's Will Grantham,' said one of the Wollaton retainers.

Edward leaned down to help the man to his feet. 'What happened?' he demanded.

Grantham waved an arm in the direction of the open gate. 'Half a dozen men were coming through there with some deer, driving them into the road. I was eating supper in the gatehouse, and I demanded to know their business. Before I could get an answer, the bastards set about me with their clubs, then opened the gate with my keys. They must be well on their way into town by now, and I doubt you could catch them.'

Of the responding curses, Edward's was the loudest. They'd been tricked — and Edward's employer would be far from impressed. The least he could do was find the person who'd fed him the information and give him a beating.

The two outrider horses cantered through the main gates of Thurland Hall, followed by the fine coach bearing its distinguished occupant. As it came to a halt in front of the Hall's magnificent front doors, two stableboys ran from their stations to take command of the two horses pulling it, while the coachman alighted and opened the passenger door. Onto the cobbles stepped a weary Robert Cecil, younger son of the illustrious Sir William Cecil, Secretary of State to Queen Elizabeth, and recently elevated to the title of Baron Burghley.

Whether the son would become as eminent as his father remained to be seen, but if physical attributes were anything to go by, this seemed unlikely. Standing at only five feet four inches in height, and with a marked curvature of the spine, Robert earned silent ridicule at court. This had done little to mellow his naturally morose and resentful nature, and he was already gaining a reputation for deviousness in matters of state as his ageing father delegated more and more tasks to him. He was journeying north on the queen's business, and it was a feather in the cap of his host, Sir John Holles, that he had opted to stay overnight in what was regarded as the finest residence in Nottingham.

Sir John raced forward to bow obsequiously and smile a welcome, while his visitor stretched his back after four hours in his coach.

'Welcome, Master Cecil. I trust that your journey from Leicester proved agreeable?'

Cecil nodded brusquely. 'The roads were passable, certainly, and the reason for that became obvious a few moments ago when we crossed that river by means of a narrow bridge. To judge by its high banks, you have had little rain of late.'

'Indeed we have not, but that is all to the good, since it is late harvest time in our orchards to the rear of the house, and I will have the honour of placing our finest stone fruits on the supper table for you to savour. But come in and refresh yourself with fine wine, to chase the chill from your bones.'

Cecil looked up admiringly at the three-storey building with its crenulated roofline. 'You have a fine house, sir, as I was advised by your neighbour Sir Francis Willoughby. I believe he once abided here.'

'He did indeed, while he awaited the completion of his grand new residence out in Wollaton. I was fortunate to be able to purchase this house from his family only last year. I am hopeful that Her Majesty will grace us with her presence when she comes to admire Wollaton Hall.'

'*If* she does, sir — *if* she does,' Cecil cautioned him. 'She grows weary of late, and has not yet fully regained her youthful vigour after seeing off the Spaniards. But let us go in; I look forward to some restful luxury.'

Cecil had chosen his overnight accommodation wisely. For the previous generation, the most obvious staging post on the road north would have been the ancient castle that sat atop the massive sandstone rock that dominated the western approaches to the town. It had been a favourite watering hole of King John several centuries in the past. Now, however, it was little more than a medieval ruin. Although it still maintained a garrison under a colonel who deputised for its absentee governor, it was hardly a suitable overnight residence for a royal emissary. His armed escort, lesser attendants and hangers-on would be required to bed down there for the night, but Robert Cecil was more needful of warmth, comfort and elevated company.

'How go things with your worthy father?' Holles asked over the rim of his goblet of mulled wine as the two men stood before the blazing log fire in the reception hall.

'For his age he is remarkably fit and well, if one discounts the occasional attack of gout that comes as the result of his rich living,' Cecil answered guardedly. 'He once dined almost nightly with Her Majesty, but he bore the brunt of her pretended wrath when the Scottish queen was executed without Elizabeth's knowledge. His banishment from court was of course a ruse only, for the sake of appearances, given his past services to Her Majesty and the ongoing need she has of his wisdom and statecraft. But he is, these days, also prone to shortness of breath during the colder months, which is why I have been sent north in his place, to deliver letters to the Scottish court. This would have been the task of Sir Francis Walsingham, were he still alive, but since his death earlier this year, such matters are increasingly devolved upon me.'

Holles thought carefully before diplomatically picking up the point. 'It is indeed said abroad that Her Majesty was most grieved by the need to execute Mary Stuart. Presumably her son bears no ill will towards our gracious monarch?'

'You seek to sound me out regarding our current relations with the Scottish king? I will say to you what I say to others who make the same enquiry. King James may well mourn the loss of a mother he never really knew, but he is also mindful that Queen Elizabeth is his distant cousin, and deserving of the respect that attends the possession of a powerful army to his south.'

'And Her Majesty thrives, despite the many plots against her throne these recent years?'

'There you tread too far, sir,' Cecil admonished him. 'I am not entrusted with my much valued work on Her Majesty's behalf because I am wont to flap at the mouth. Quite the contrary. I'll say only that Her Majesty feels her advancing years, as would any grand dame who is approaching her sixtieth birthday. However, thanks in no small part to my father's excellent guidance and undying loyalty, her grip upon her throne remains as strong as it ever was.'

'But she remains childless,' Holles reminded him. 'Does your journey north relate to the matter of succession?'

Cecil glared back in the manner that could normally be relied upon to freeze men to the marrow. 'That would have been one question too many, had it been asked. But I shall assume that it was not, if we might now progress to our supper.'

2

'Give me one good reason why I shouldn't beat your brains out!' Edward bellowed as he grabbed Francis Barton by the collar of his doublet and all but lifted him off the floor. They were in the house that they shared in Whitefriars Lane, close to the old castle.

Francis looked down at Edward's gnarled fist. 'For one thing, I'm bigger than you. I'm also older and more wily when it comes to fisticuffs. And for good measure, I'm bailiff to the Sheriff of Nottingham, and not even your status as bailiff to the county sheriff will preserve you from being taken up for assault. Now, calm down and tell me what's wrong.'

Francis had several persuasive points. He was indeed Edward's contemporary in law enforcement, as bailiff to the town sheriff. The two men shared the house that had originally been built for the town bailiff, and as its contribution the county paid the meagre wage of Dickon, the servant who looked after the house and cooked the bailiffs' meals. Both men remained unmarried, and had become friendly despite the rivalry between the two sheriffdoms, although they would occasionally compete in a gentlemanly way for the right to investigate a matter that was on the borderline of their adjoining jurisdictions. Sometimes they even worked in tandem, although the suspicion of underhanded dealing by one against the other was never far below the surface.

Edward relaxed his grip and took a deep breath. 'Your information caused me to spend a most uncomfortable evening skulking in the undergrowth of Wollaton Park like a rat seeking a hole. I had to take many of the estate's outdoor workers with me, and while we were catching our death of cold in the freezing fog down by the lake, the deer we were supposed to be guarding were being driven off through the far gate by the very thieves we were supposed to be apprehending. All on the basis of *your* advice, of course. So own up — who put you up to it?'

Francis looked genuinely shocked. 'Are you suggesting that I deliberately sent you in the opposite direction so that the thieves could get away with poaching deer? Have you forgotten that I'm a bailiff like yourself, dedicated to upholding the Queen's Peace? If it had been taking place in the town, I'd have been acting on the information myself.'

'There aren't many deer in the town, though, are there? Everything to the west of here — including that ruin of a castle — is under my jurisdiction.'

'Strictly speaking, it's under the jurisdiction of the sheriff,' Francis pointed out. 'Don't get above yourself.'

'Don't change the subject!' Edward shouted. 'If it wasn't your clever trick to get everyone out of the way, then whose was it?'

'It was Billy Sneddon who told me what was being planned for yesterday, at around sunset, he reckoned.'

'And who's he? Tell me where he lives, so that I can kick him stupid before I run him into the Shire Hall cells.'

'He's just a labourer, although he likes to call himself a carrier. You won't be any more pleased to learn that what he carries are meat carcasses. He works for Alderman Brackenridge, the butcher on Timber Hill, just up the road there. It's a convenient distance from the marketplace.'

'And from where did *his* information come?'

'No idea. Perhaps you'd like to ask him yourself, but bear in mind that if you do him any violence, I'll be obliged to run you into the Guildhall, where the town authorities maintain a set of gaol cells. They're slightly inferior to those of the county in the Shire Hall.'

'I might try his employer first,' said Edward.

Francis shook his head. 'A word to the wise. Henry Brackenridge is one of the most important and influential men in this town. He's a personal friend of both Sir Francis Willoughby and Sir John Holles, and if rumour be correct he's likely to become our next mayor. It's also rumoured that he has his eye on becoming our next town sheriff, so I may be working under his command before long.'

'If that was meant to impress me, or divert me from my duty, then it failed,' Edward snorted. 'You forget that when I was a soldier I mixed with much more elevated nobles than your local hacker of dead animals. The Earl of Leicester, for one.'

'Here we go again,' Francis sighed. 'You never tire of telling me how he recommended you for the position of bailiff to the county sheriff. So how did you earn yourself such a good opinion of the queen's favourite? Covering up his fumbles in the royal bedchamber?'

Edward laughed, and the atmosphere became less tense. 'If I repeated what you just said in the appropriate quarter, you'd be kicking the air on Tower Hill.'

'Now that you appear to have calmed down,' Francis said, 'Dickon boiled some pork for supper, and he baked fresh bread.'

'At least there's one person in this place I can rely on,' Edward grumbled as he walked out to the water butt to wash his hands.

The following morning, still peeved, he was awoken by the strident sound of a woman giving Francis her opinion of his abilities. Since it wasn't very complimentary, Edward concluded that it would make as good a start to the day as any, and wandered out into the main room in his undershirt and hose. The woman eyed him with distaste, then glared back at Francis.

'Who might you be?' Edward asked the woman.

She drew herself up to her full height. 'I'm Rose Franklin, cook to Sir John Holles, up at Thurland Hall. Not that it's any of your business.'

'This gentleman is bailiff to the county sheriff,' Francis explained. 'It would be helpful to narrate your grievance to him as well, since your errant daughter may well have slipped beyond the town boundaries in her desire to get away from you.'

Rose's face turned the same colour as her name. 'You brazen pox-monger! She's a biddable girl, is my Nell, and she's never been known to wander far from our hearth before, which is what makes me think something bad has overtaken her. She was meant to be working with me in the master's kitchens yesterday, since we had an important visitor up from London, but she never turned up. I've been so busy preparing for a banquet over the past few days that I haven't been home for a day or two, so I didn't know that Nell's been missing for four days altogether.'

'And where did you last know her to be?' Francis asked.

Rose shrugged. 'I've no idea, to be totally honest with you. She works most of the time in that there washhouse in Bridlesmith Gate, but she does lots of house calls delivering the finished clothes. I've been told she was last seen delivering to a house in High Pavement. But that was four days ago, like I said.'

'I'll make enquiries when I do my rounds,' Francis promised, 'but no doubt my friend here, Edward Mountsorrel, can also ask if anyone's seen her out in the county somewhere.'

'What does she look like?' Edward asked.

'She's a tall lass, and well built, with long fair hair that she piles on top of her head under a bonnet, just to look like more of a lady than she is. Everybody round the town knows her by sight.'

'But not necessarily everyone *out of* town,' said Edward. 'It's a pity she's been gone for several days without anyone noticing. Do you think her father could give us any more information?'

'Not once the alehouses are open,' Rose replied with a snarl. 'If he'd been looking after her the way he should have been, she wouldn't be missing. I bet *your* father kept a better eye on you.'

'I'm an orphan,' Edward told her.

Rose blustered to overcome her embarrassment. 'There's no shame in that, but at least you were properly supervised.'

'I was until I escaped at the age of fifteen,' said Edward. 'I lived by my wits after that, until I became a soldier.'

'Well, Nell doesn't have much in the way of wits,' Rose told him sadly. 'Anyway, I've got my own duties to attend to. The visitor at Thurland Hall will no doubt be wanting to fill his face with the roast venison I left for the kitchen boy to turn on the spit.'

'Venison?' Edward asked, his interest tweaked. 'Is that a normal dish where you work? Who do you work for again?'

'Sir John Holles, and no — we don't normally have venison. But we've got a special visitor from London — someone close to the queen, they reckon — and we got the venison specially.'

'Who's your butcher?' Edward asked with a sidelong glance at Francis.

'Brackenridge, from up near the market,' she replied. 'He's a good friend of the master, seemingly.'

As Rose made her way out of the house, Edward turned to Francis. 'I will definitely start with this Brackenridge person, and I don't give a damn who his friends may be. It's too much of a coincidence to ignore.'

'While you do that, I'll start on the alehouses,' said Francis.

Edward raised an eyebrow. 'A bit early in the day for that sort of thing, isn't it?'

'Not for myself, you addle-brain. In search of Nell Franklin. Her mother may not know it, or be prepared to admit it, but Nell's one of the better class prostitutes around the town. The laundry delivery's just a cover for what she's *really* taking down to the fancy houses, when the lady of the house is absent. It's well known among the so-called "better" classes of Nottingham that if you require Nell's services, you leave your order at the washhouse, whose proprietor takes a cut of Nell's earnings.'

'If she's so selective, why are you planning to make enquiries about her in the local alehouses?'

'Because all prostitutes, regardless of how they pursue their trade, like to enjoy each other's company at the end of a working day. There are certain alehouse landlords who welcome their money, and even hire out a room or two for their activities.'

'How do you happen to know all this?' Edward asked.

Francis tapped the side of his nose. 'Prostitutes are useful sources of information. I know what they do for a living, and they know that I know, so in return for my not handing them over to the constables, they're happy to talk. If a local labourer, or modestly placed tradesman, suddenly has enough money to enjoy the services of a prostitute, I'd like to know about it, because that money may have been obtained unlawfully. On this occasion, I might learn something of Nell Franklin's recent whereabouts. At the very least I can tell her mother that she's still alive.'

'And will you also tell her how her daughter goes about earning extra money?'

'What do *you* think? You met the lady — I wouldn't want to be the one to tell her that her daughter's a prostitute. In any case, we might need her assistance in learning whether that venison came from the Wollaton estate. If there are stolen deer being eaten at the tables of the high and mighty here in Nottingham, then I need to know about it.'

'Will you then arrest Sir John Holles?' Edward asked.

Francis shook his head. 'He's too well connected, I'm afraid. That visitor he's currently entertaining is rumoured to be none other than Robert Cecil.'

'The son of the Secretary of State, Sir William Cecil?'

'The very same. I received orders from my employer yesterday to keep the streets approaching Thurland Hall clear of beggars and cut-throats, and he intimated as much. It seems that Cecil's on his way north on the queen's business.'

'But what if I discover that Holles did indeed take venison into his kitchen, knowing where it had come from?' asked Edward.

'Tell me, if you do. I'll tell my employer, and *he* can decide what to do.'

'Good luck with that. I'll start at the other end of the chain, working backwards from the man who delivered the carcasses to Thurland Hall.'

An hour later, Edward was doing just that. After a few minutes standing by the gates that led from the yard of Brackenridge's Butchery, he stepped smartly to the side of a cart that was leaving and took hold of the horse's bridle, bringing the load to a halt.

'What's your game?' its driver demanded.

'Billy Sneddon?' Edward asked.

'Who wants to know?'

'Me. I'm Edward Mountsorrel, bailiff to the Sheriff of Nottinghamshire.'

'Congratulations. Now get out of my way, and let go of that horse.'

'All in good time, Master Sneddon. I'm here to enquire about certain information you gave to the town bailiff, Francis Barton. Remember him?'

'Of course I do — he does your job, doesn't he?'

'Not quite, but as good as. He tells me that you gave him certain information regarding a planned poaching operation in Wollaton Park yesterday evening. Would that be correct?'

'Yes — so what?'

'The information was false. While I and a few assistants were watching the exit from the deer park that I was told would be used, the poachers got away with several head of deer from the far exit.'

'It wasn't your day then, was it?'

'And it won't be yours either, if you don't tell me who gave you the information in the first place. For all I know, you were one of the poachers. Do you know what they do to those caught poaching?'

'It weren't me, honest!' Sneddon whined. 'I were just told to pass the information on by somebody else!'

'And who might that have been?'

'I can't tell you. I'll lose my job.'

'If you don't, you may lose your life, you cretin! Which is it to be — your job or your neck?'

'It was my boss,' Sneddon admitted, white in the face. He jerked his head towards the yard at the rear. 'Master Brackenridge.'

'See how easy it is to save your neck from the noose?' said Edward as he let go of the horse's bridle. 'Off you go with your no doubt poisonous load. I worked on an estate once in my early years, and to judge by the colour of those sides of lamb, anyone who eats them will be dead by the following morning.'

Sneddon flicked the reins, and the horse plodded forward. Edward walked down the alleyway, holding his breath until he was beside the man who was shouting orders to the other carters. He looked up as he saw Edward standing there, and gave him a smile that was as broad as it was insincere.

'You wish to place an order, good sir?'

'No, I wish to ask you a very important question.'

'All my produce is fresh, if that's your question.'

'Fresh, no doubt, when it first arrives here, but to judge by the smell, it's outstayed its welcome by the time it leaves.'

'Are you from the town authorities? If so, I'll have you know that you're talking to an alderman.'

'This I know,' Edward smiled indulgently. 'Alderman Brackenridge, correct?'

'The very same. And since you appear to have the advantage of me, who might you be?'

'Edward Mountsorrel, bailiff to the Sheriff of Nottinghamshire.'

'My good friend Thomas Thornhough? How go matters with him?'

'They'll go much better when I'm able to advise him who fed me certain false information regarding the activities of poachers on the Wollaton estate.'

'And how might I assist in that?'

'By admitting that it was you, for a start. Then you can tell me how you acquired that information.'

'I certainly passed certain information to the town bailiff, Master Francis Barton.'

'And he passed it on to me, because Wollaton lies well into the county, as you must know for yourself. The information led me and several estate retainers to watch one end of the deer park while the deer were stolen from the other end.'

'You say that the information was false?'

'I do, so why should I not suspect you of being in league with the poachers? After all, you stand to gain much by having a cheap source of venison.'

'You accuse *me*? How *dare* you voice such a slander! I shall lose no time in reporting your manner, and your false accusations, to your employer, and my *very* good friend, the sheriff!'

'Feel free to do so, since it will save me reporting your involvement. Might I also ask whether or not it was you who supplied venison to Thurland Hall for consumption at today's dinner table?'

'I'm proud to advise you that I have the honour of supplying the meats for the table of Sir John Holles and his family, certainly. He's well connected and aspires to become the next county sheriff, which will of course make you accountable directly to him. You should therefore have a care over how you try to connect him with stolen venison.'

'I don't recall claiming that the venison *was* stolen,' Edward replied with satisfaction. 'But you have obviously made the same connection as I. Deer go missing from the Wollaton estate one day, and lo and behold the town's leading butcher is able to supply venison for the table of an upper-class citizen the following day.'

'Outrageous!' Brackenridge bellowed. 'Leave my premises at once, or else…'

'Or else what? You'll report me to the sheriff?'

'You arrogant upstart! How can you accuse one of the town's leading citizens of a vulgar crime such as poaching? My only motive was to preserve the herd of my good friend Sir Francis Willoughby, who owns and maintains the Wollaton estate, which is shortly to be graced with a visit by Her Majesty.'

'You are clearly well blessed with friends,' said Edward, unconcerned by the man's boasted connections. 'If you were so anxious to protect the interests of the man you claim as a "good friend", why did you not advise him directly of the threat of poachers? Why rely on the good offices of the sheriff, even though you appear to have selected the wrong one?'

'It was Sir Francis himself who advised me of the threat to his herd, and asked that I alert the appropriate authority.'

'Why could he not do that himself?'

'Perhaps you might care to ask such an arrogant question of the man himself,' Brackenridge suggested. 'Assuming that you can get past his pack of hounds, he would no doubt have you set upon by his sturdy retainers and thrown back onto the public road that adjoins his estate.'

'Those very retainers had their time wasted in the fruitless pursuit of poachers, as a result of your deceptive information. They appeared to be as ignorant of the matter as I had been prior to my town colleague passing on what you had said. You say that you were asked to do that by Sir Francis himself?'

'Indeed I do,' Brackenridge insisted. 'He had come into possession of that information — by what means, I have no idea — and he asked that I alert the sheriff.'

'He did not specify which sheriff?'

'No, of course not. How was he to know who was the appropriate one, any more than I?'

'I would have thought that your close friendship with the county sheriff would have led you to seek him out personally and pass on your valuable information,' Edward said with a slow smile. 'Instead, you left it to a man whose talents extend only to driving around your carts of overripe meat to inform the *town* sheriff. By this means you were able to claim, if challenged, that you had done what was required of you by your *other* "dear friend" Sir Francis, while at the same time doing your best to ensure that the information went no further — certainly not far enough for the poachers to be caught. Did Sir Francis, by any chance, also advise you of which end of the park was destined to have the deer removed from it?'

'You should leave,' Brackenridge told him coldly, 'otherwise you will have *my* dogs to contend with.'

'I suspect that they are attracted only to meat that is long past its best,' said Edward as he turned to leave. 'I'd like to thank you for your assistance, but I'm not sure you gave me any. Not knowingly, anyway. Good day to you.'

3

A deathly silence fell among those gathered in the taproom of The Dog and Partridge, perched awkwardly on the slope of Hollow Stone, as Francis Barton walked in. He looked round at the apprehensive faces. 'I'm not here to stop your fun and games, even though it's not yet noon and you should be about a more lawful purpose,' he reassured them. 'I'm looking for someone.'

'There's enough of us to choose from,' replied Lily Carter, an older woman. 'I imagine that a lusty young man like you might appreciate something a bit different.'

'No offence, Lily,' Francis replied, 'but when I said I was looking for someone, I meant Nell Franklin.'

'Well, when you find her, remind her that she owes me a shilling,' chimed in Tilley Chandler. 'She can afford to pay me back, now that she's found herself a fine gentleman. They're off to London in a fine coach.'

'She's left for London?'

Tilley shrugged. 'I don't know if she's left yet, but that was what she was bragging about the last time she deigned to come here. That must have been three nights or more ago, and she promised to pay me back before she left. We haven't seen her since, so I'm hoping she hasn't gone yet. Of course, if you'd like to pay her debt, I could see you right in the back room.'

'Where would she be staying before leaving for London?' Francis asked eagerly. 'Her mother hasn't seen her for four days now.'

'Goodness knows,' said Lily, 'but you can't blame her for leaving that rat-pit of a house, with a father who's drunk all day. Good luck to her, that's what I say.'

'So none of you can give me any more information about where she might be found, who with, and when she might have departed the town for her new life?' Francis asked as he gazed round at the faces of the town doxies.

'You might try The Crusader,' Jenny Salter offered. 'She often worked that place, because she reckoned you get a better class of client in there — the men from the castle, among others. I always found them too rough, but they pay well.'

'Her new fellow was called Richard,' Tilley added. 'If you were to believe what she was bragging about, he's *Sir* Richard, and he's got a house near the river in London that he's been keeping for the right woman.'

'I don't suppose you can tell me his second name?' Francis ventured.

'How long have you been a bailiff? You must know that the sort of business we conduct doesn't require any second names,' said Lily. 'You could call yourself "King Doodle" for all we care, if the money's good.'

'But you reckon that Nell was meeting this man in The Crusader?' Francis persevered.

Jenny nodded. 'It's that place just below the castle rock, across from the Leen, if you don't know it. It's a bit damp and smelly on account of the river, but they say that the upstairs rooms is comfortable enough. I might try it myself one night, because Nell isn't the only one who's struck it lucky down there.'

'Other women have found men to take them down to London, you mean?'

'Don't know about London,' Jenny replied thoughtfully, 'but a couple of nights ago, Annie Freebourne was sporting a new bonnet that she said had been bought by this man she'd done the business with. Apparently he wanted to take her back with him to some castle or other down south. Might've been London, if they've got castles down there. If so, I hope for her sake that it's not as draughty as that ruin we've got.'

'So what you're telling me is that two of your friends have recently met wealthy men in this alehouse called The Crusader, and have been talked into leaving town with them?'

'You make it sound a bit chancy,' another young woman piped up. 'Are you saying that they might've been dragged away and had horrible things done to them?'

A raucous laugh from Lily Carter ended that line of enquiry. 'Easy to see you haven't been in this game for long, sweetheart. I get horrible things done to me every night, but I make sure I get paid properly for it. So what's a woman got to lose by finding someone who'll keep her fed and housed in exchange for her services? At least she won't have to find her own clients in future.'

'Well, thank you anyway, ladies,' Francis smiled as he turned to leave. 'I'll see if I can find the men who are looking to entice sexual partners down to a fine life in London.'

They hadn't set the dogs on him the last time he'd been in Wollaton Park, so Edward approached the hut of the herd-master, Amos Blunt. Amos looked up from the knife he was sharpening and scowled.

'If you were thinking about getting us all out there again on our knees in the fog, forget it,' he growled.

Edward smiled. 'Not today — I'm still getting the feeling back in my toes. Today I'm here to speak to your master.'

'Sir Francis? You'll be lucky. He doesn't speak to anybody unless they're nobility, and anyway, he's out inspecting one of his coalmines.'

'When is he expected back?'

'No idea. I suggest you ask in the kitchen — round past the rose garden, and then up the path. Did you get the poachers?'

'Not yet, but I've a good idea where the venison finished up. That's why I'm here, but you can help me on that point. What was the first warning you had that there were going to be poachers after the deer?'

'When you turned up. You're not the most popular man around these parts, I should warn you.'

'Sir Francis said nothing to you, or anyone else, about poachers?'

'Not to me. Why do you ask?'

'Because someone in the town tried to persuade me that the warning about poachers came from Sir Francis himself, and I'm rather keen on proving that man to be a liar.'

'If the master knew all about it, he'd have left it to the estate workers to catch them at it. He wouldn't have called in the sheriff and his bailiff. And with the greatest of respect, we'd have made a better job of it left to our own devices. We wouldn't have put all our men down by the lake, for one thing. Meaning no offence, and all that.'

'None taken, but it makes you think, doesn't it?' Edward mused. 'I came here with information that suggested that the vale gate was the one that would be used, which meant that we were all as far away as possible from the Derby Road gate when the beasts were driven out.'

'We were all deliberately misled, you mean?'

'Yes, precisely. Sir Francis would have known better how his beasts could be stolen, and he wouldn't have concentrated all his men in one spot.'

Amos grinned. 'Last I heard, the master was threatening to complain to your boss. Seems that they're the best of friends, and I won't repeat what he was calling you.'

'Thank you for that, at least,' Edward replied wryly. 'I'll take myself up to the kitchen, since the sooner I get this over with, the better. Round past the rose garden, you said?'

'Close that door!' a florid-faced lady yelled from beneath her starched cap as Edward stood uncertainly in the kitchen doorway. He deduced that she was the cook. 'Were you born in a barn? These pie crusts will never rise if you let the cold draught in!'

There were several other people in the kitchen, and Edward turned as he sensed someone slipping behind him to close the door in response to the cook's irate command. He found himself gazing into an entrancing pair of light hazel eyes, and he mumbled his thanks before allowing himself to take in the rest of the obliging young lady. She certainly wasn't a member of the kitchen staff, to judge by her elegant blue velvet gown and the matching wired hood.

'What's your business?' the cook demanded, stirring vigorously. 'We get all our poultry from the village, and the master doesn't care for fish, so what are you selling?'

'I'm here to speak to your master,' Edward persevered. 'I'm Edward Mountsorrel, bailiff to the county sheriff.'

'Have you come with the sheriff himself? I'm Betsy Tinker, the cook, and I wasn't told to expect visitors for dinner.'

'No, I'm here on my own account,' Edward explained, 'making further enquiries about the deer that were poached from the estate yesterday.'

Betsy snorted. 'If I were you, I'd go back out, then come back in wearing one of those tin hats that they wear on the battlefield. If you are who I think you are, the master's after your blood.'

'So I've been advised. I wouldn't be here if I didn't have an important question for your master.'

'That's as may be, but you're in my way. I'm supposed to be feeding the household staff, but it's going to be another few minutes before anything's ready, so go outside. Maybe young Beth will be obliging enough to take you for a turn around the rose garden.'

Beth — the young woman who'd closed the kitchen door behind him — sidled up to Edward with a smile that made his head spin, and performed a half curtsy. 'I'd be more than happy to do that,' she purred. Once they had left the kitchen, she introduced herself. 'I'm Elizabeth Porter, lady's maid to Bridget Willoughby, the master's eldest daughter. She also married a Willoughby, so she had no need to change her name.'

'As you already heard,' Edward murmured as he breathed in the smell of the rose bushes around them, 'my name is Edward Mountsorrel, and I'm bailiff to the county sheriff. I'm investigating the theft of some deer from the estate.'

'From what I've heard, you were the cause of it,' Elizabeth chided him with a smile. 'The master was very angry that he'd been robbed. He wasn't concerned about the loss of the deer — more the fact that he'd been bested, and let down by a man he regards as a good friend of his.'

'My employer? I'm not sure who I dread facing most — your master or the sheriff, although it wasn't really my fault. We were tricked into being in the wrong place by someone who was clearly part of the wicked scheme. However, I'll take some delight in advising Sir Francis that his deer may have finished up on the table of another good friend of his.'

'The deer weren't important to him,' said Elizabeth. 'He's only interested in his coalmines — the nasty black stuff that makes all that smoke when we burn it in the fireplaces instead of honest wood. Let's take this left-hand path, shall we? It will bring us back to the front door in due course. You'll need to allow me to take your arm as we step over these dividing stones.'

They were many yards into the long path that ran through the middle of two high lines of bushes before she dropped her hand from his arm, seemingly with reluctance. 'Would that the path were rougher,' Edward murmured, and she immediately took his arm again.

'You must think me a little forward,' she whispered, 'but it's so reassuring to have a man's arm to hold onto in these dangerous times.'

'Is it dangerous for you here on the estate?' Edward asked in disbelief.

Elizabeth shook her head. 'Not usually, but out there in the wider world, that's a different matter, so they advise me. On the estate we occasionally get vagabonds wandering about in search of game birds, which they capture in those awful snares. It was much worse where I was raised in Leicestershire, on the la Zouche estate in Ashby, where my father was the steward. Gangs of poachers would come out from Leicester and drive off the cattle from the lower fields, and more than one herdsman was left for dead when they tried to stop them. But since I am from Leicestershire, I am interested in your family name. "Mountsorrel" — did I hear correctly?'

'You did indeed, Mistress Porter.'

'Please — you must call me Elizabeth.'

'Not Beth?'

'Not if you wish to please me. "Beth" is the demeaning name by which I am known to the Willoughby family, as if I am not fit to go by the same name as our queen.'

'Then I shall of course call you Elizabeth, and thank you for the privilege. But what is it about my name that you find of interest?'

'Mountsorrel I know to be a village in Leicestershire. Are you the son of the lord of the manor there?'

Edward burst out laughing, then asked Elizabeth's pardon. 'In truth I am an orphan, and Mountsorrel was the village in which I was found abandoned in 1563. I was left in the doorway of the local parish church, in the hope that Christian charity would prevail, as indeed it did. I was taken by the local clergyman to Wigston Hospital, an almshouse for the destitute. They named me after the village of my abandonment, if not my birth, and they added the first name "Edward", since they had no other child of that name in the dormitory. I was taught to read and write a little, and set to work in the fields where they grew the crops with which we were fed. I made use of that training when I ran away at the age of fifteen and found work in the grounds of the former Grey estate at Groby.'

'But it was not your skill in growing cabbages that qualified you to serve the county sheriff?' Elizabeth asked.

'Indeed not. It was while preserving the estate from marauding bands of vagabonds that I learned I had a certain ability with my fists and — if you would forgive my pretension — my wits. I wondered if I might make my fortune from them, and to that end I joined the local Trained Band for the county. I worked my way up to the rank of captain, then when the Earl of Leicester called all the Trained Bands down to Tilbury to defend England against the Armada I found favour with him. Once the Spanish were defeated at sea and the Trained Bands were disbanded, I was sent back north to Thomas Thornhough, the Sheriff of Nottinghamshire, with a letter of recommendation. I have been in his service these past nine months. But enough of me — what of yourself, if I might make so bold?'

Elizabeth sighed. 'Nothing so exciting as your life, I'm afraid. I was brought up on an estate, taught by both parents how to disport myself in polite society, and then sent out as a lady's maid. The la Zouche family had many business interests, one of which was the development of those ugly coalmines, and by this means my family's employer knew the Willoughby family. My mother was the la Zouches' housekeeper, in charge of the maids, and she had taught me all that she knew. Then one day when the Willoughbys were visiting, it was announced that their daughter Bridget was about to marry a distant cousin. I was asked to attend upon her while she was measured for her wedding gown by a dressmaker from Leicester. We seemed to be suited, so she requested that my parents release me into her service, and here I am.'

'Do your duties permit you to have any life of your own?' Edward asked.

Elizabeth looked down, choosing her words carefully. 'I am allowed to pursue my own interests when I am not required by my mistress. My love of the open air has remained with me since my days in Leicestershire, where the breezes were as fresh and sweet as they are here. But, as I said earlier, I grow fearful of the many ruffians who seem to regard the rolling acres here as theirs to plunder for the wildlife, so I rarely proceed beyond where we are walking now.'

'Surely the estate has men who could accompany you?'

Elizabeth looked into Edward's eyes as she replied, 'It would not be seemly for a lady's maid to be seen walking with a retainer who works outdoors, and the master is very particular about matters such as that. He is strict about the observance of etiquette and appropriate manners. But now I see that we have come to the end of the walk, and must turn back to the main house.'

'Before we do so, might I be so bold as to suggest that I could be a suitable companion for any future walk you might wish to take through the grounds?'

'Indeed you might,' she replied coyly. 'But do not your duties keep you away from here?'

'Nothing would stop me from walking, as I have done today, with such an attractive and charming companion.'

'Then consider it a suitable arrangement for another day. My usual half day is a Wednesday, should you be free on Wednesday next. Do not trouble yourself to call at the hall itself — simply make your way to the rose garden where we began our walk today. And now here we are — may I say what a pleasure this past half hour has been for me?'

'For me also,' Edward replied.

At that moment, there was a flurry of action at the foot of the steps leading up to the front doors of the hall. A coach pulled up and a coachman stepped down from his box to open its door. At the same time there was the sound of loud barking as two hounds bounded up the grassy slope towards Edward and Elizabeth.

Edward instinctively drew his sword and stepped in front of Elizabeth in a defensive gesture as the two hounds began growling and salivating. There was a shout to call them off, and as they retreated a red-faced man dressed in morning finery strode towards them.

'Who the devil might you be, sir, to threaten my dogs in that rude manner?'

'They were about to attack this lady by my side,' Edward offered by way of explanation. 'Not to mention myself.'

'They are trained to attack intruders such as yourself, so I ask again — who might you be?'

'Edward Mountsorrel, bailiff to the county sheriff.'

'The fool who lost me four of my best deer? I should have let the dogs have you. As for you, Mistress Porter, no doubt your mistress requires your services before supper. Off you go, and do not let me see you keeping such low company in future.'

Elizabeth scuttled off, red-faced and with her eyes cast down, while Edward remained defiantly where he was, earning an angry scowl from the man with the dogs. In the uneasy silence, Edward opted to take the initiative.

'Do I address the lord of this estate?'

'You do indeed — Sir Francis Willoughby, he who is deprived of his deer thanks to your incompetence. I have already sent a note to my good friend the sheriff expressing my displeasure at your ineptitude, so there is no need for me to repeat it. Leave my land immediately, or my dogs will rip you apart.'

'I am here in connection with the theft of your deer, sir,' Edward persisted, 'and if you will permit me, I have several questions, the answers to which will assist in identifying those responsible.'

'I will answer one question only, then I must repair to the Hall. So ask it, then be gone.'

'Did you by any chance send warning via the local town butcher Henry Brackenridge that there was to be an attack on your deer yesterday evening?'

'Of course I didn't, you numbskull! If I had known of the threat, I would have better organised our defences against it. What possesses you to ask such an idiotic question?'

'Merely that Henry Brackenridge, who was the one responsible for alerting me, claims that he was passing on a warning from you.'

'Preposterous! Do you now seek to divert the blame to a man whose acquaintance I value? Do you seek to add false accusation to the list of your transgressions?'

'I can only speak truth, sir, and I had that from the lips of Alderman Brackenridge in person. However, if it is of any consolation, I believe I know where your deer were destined for. I can perhaps prove this if you would answer one more question.'

'One more, then definitely no more.'

'Do you brand your deer?'

'Of course. If they are stolen, we may identify them by the brands on their rumps. It is a "W", to denote the Willoughby name as well as the Wollaton estate.'

'Thank you, sir — that will assist my enquiries considerably, assuming that your venison is not already fully consumed.'

'Be gone, and do not re-appear at Wollaton until you have purged your original incompetence.'

Edward was smiling to himself as he untied his horse from the post at the kitchen door and led it down through the park towards the Derby Road gate. He had expected no less from the bad-tempered owner of the Wollaton estate, but hopefully he would have an excuse to return next Wednesday to renew his acquaintance with the alluring Mistress Porter. All in all, a useful morning's work. Now to see how Francis had fared.

4

'What doesn't get eaten tonight goes into the breakfast potage,' Dickon told Edward and Francis as he placed the leftover pork on the table, along with the previous day's leftover bread. 'You men seem to have lost your appetites of late.'

'The burdens of office,' Edward remarked as he carved a chunk from the cold roast and held it up for inspection on the end of his knife. 'I hope this did not come from Brackenridge's slaughterhouse down the road.'

'I shall only have resort to his produce should I feel the need to poison you both,' said Dickon as he poured the men's beer. He then retreated to his kitchen, which had been built in the garden to minimise the risk to the house itself should there be a fire.

'So how went your enquiries of Alderman Brackenridge?' Francis asked as he cut a slice of bread.

Edward snorted. 'Apart from learning that he runs a most unsavoury meat business, and that he clearly regards himself as a man of some importance in this town, I found out very little. However, he was clearly behind the false information regarding the poaching of deer that was fed to you by his cart driver.'

'For what purpose?' Francis asked.

'The obvious one, I believe. By this means he was able to acquire a supply of venison, which according to Holles's cook may well have been sold on to feed Robert Cecil — or is it "Sir" Robert Cecil these days?'

'If that is not his title already, it will be soon. Rumour has it that he is heavily involved in his father's devious schemes now that he is in official disgrace at court, and Walsingham has died. But do you intend to pursue the matter further, and prove that the son of the eminent father dined on venison stolen from the Wollaton estate?'

'I do, and I believe I can,' said Edward. 'I learned three important things when I visited the estate earlier today. The first is that Sir Francis Willoughby is an arrogant sort who regards himself as so far above the common man that he is entitled to set his dogs on them. The second is that — contrary to what Alderman Brackenridge sought to persuade me — it was not Sir Francis who was the source of the false information, and that makes sense. Why would a man seek to draw attention to the alleged theft of his own deer? Should he have wished to make a present of them to Holles and Robert Cecil, he would have done so with great show. He would not have schemed to have them purloined from his estate by a motley crew of cut-throats.'

'And what was the third thing that you learned?' Francis asked.

Edward blushed. 'Sir Francis employs, as lady-in-waiting to his daughter Bridget, most delectable young maid you ever laid eyes upon. She and I shall, I hope, be pursuing our acquaintance in circumstances that will also allow me to observe the Wollaton estate. But how did you fare with your enquiries regarding the missing Nell Franklin?'

'I learned next to nothing, other than reminding myself that women such as her are easy prey for the wealthy and privileged. The women I spoke to could only tell me that she has fallen in with a wealthy gentleman who intends to install her in a house in London, there to use her for his sexual convenience. Sadly, her friends at the alehouse seemed to regard this as an improvement in her fortunes. And she is seemingly not the only one — there is another such doxy named Annie Freebourne, who has similarly been lured down south with the promise of food and shelter in return for her exclusive favours.'

'By the same man?'

'I was not so informed, nor is it likely, if you consider the matter for a moment. If you had constant access to one woman for all your sexual needs, would you need a second?'

'Many a married man has done so,' Edward replied.

'Be that as it may, I must assume that the two young women were seduced south by two different men. The difficulty I face is explaining to Rose Franklin that her daughter has become the mistress of some wealthy London merchant.'

'You will tell her such?'

'I can hardly tell her that I have done nothing in response to her request for my assistance,' Francis argued, 'so I must tell her what I have learned. Given what I have heard of life in the Franklin household, she may even be persuaded that her precious daughter has gone up in the world.'

'Would you rather that I tell her?'

Francis looked at Edward in surprise. 'Why would you undertake such an unpleasant task? And would she be likely to believe you, given that I am the town bailiff and the task was entrusted to me? Although there *is* a connection with the county, in that both Nell and Annie are said to have met their gentleman protectors in an alehouse under the castle rock. It had some religious name, as I recall.'

'The Crusader?' Edward asked with a grimace.

Francis nodded. 'The very same. You know it?'

'Regrettably I do. It is the resort of every low malefactor to the west of the town, and a good many from within it. The proprietor brews his own ale, and the water is rumoured to come from the nearby Leen, which is also the source of much local pestilence. The Crusader might well be the sort of place in which a lusty old merchant would seek a prostitute, if properly advised. To add to the undesirability of the place, it is popular with soldiers from the castle that sits above it. When fights break out in its main room, one would need an army of one's own to break them up.'

'I think you have persuaded me that you are the bailiff best placed to make enquiries in The Crusader regarding the likely fate of Nell Franklin,' said Francis.

Edward nodded. 'I will do so, if you would do something for me.'

'What, pray?'

'You are intending to visit Thurland Hall in order to speak to Rose Franklin regarding your enquiries?'

'Indeed. What is it you require of me while I am there?'

'Something else I learned while out at Wollaton is that the deer on that estate were branded with the letter "W". If there be anything left of the beasts stolen from there — perhaps in Mistress Franklin's larder — then it should be possible to identify them as having been stolen from Sir Francis.'

Francis looked troubled. 'We must proceed with caution, I suggest, should that be the case. Sir John Holles is better connected than Alderman Brackenridge, and possibly Sir Francis Willoughby. We must pause and think carefully before we accuse Sir John of purchasing stolen deer, and Robert Cecil of consuming it.'

Edward shook his head vigorously. 'We are sworn to uphold the law without fear or favour, are we not?'

'We are also dependent on the good opinions of our employers,' Francis pointed out, 'and we are responsible to ourselves for the continued presence of our heads on our shoulders. I can think of nothing more likely to hazard them than a wild accusation that the son of the queen's secretary was dining on stolen venison.'

'But we are not proposing to allege that he knew of the source of that venison, are we?' Edward argued. 'If his host saw fit to impress him by serving him a fine roast for his dinner, how might his guest be said to have been complicit in its dishonest origins?'

'I merely pass on to you a caution born of my experience as a constable in this town, before I was elevated to bailiff. It is not a matter of what you know, but *who* you know, and what use you make of your knowledge. There are times when it is more expedient to remain silent, and simply use your acquired knowledge for your own purposes.'

Edward's jaw dropped. 'If we judge men according to who they are, and what positions of authority they occupy, rather than what foul deeds they may have committed, then we do not uphold the law. We merely apply it for the wrong reasons, turning a blind eye to crimes that we should be reporting.'

Francis's response was a derisory laugh. 'You clearly have not learned much of the history of this nation. I could name men much more elevated in society than ourselves who lost everything because of their stubborn consciences and their insistence on the so-called truth. 'The "truth", my friend, is whatever it is wise to reveal at any given time, and I for one am not about to expose myself to calumny, disgrace, loss of office and possible death, for the sake of a handful of deer.'

'Will you at least enquire after possible brand marks on the rumps of any remaining deer in the larder of Thurland Hall, while I make enquiries in The Crusader?'

'I will certainly go that far,' Francis agreed. 'But beyond that, you may be working alone.'

'I would rather do that than work alongside a man whose service of the law is so easily diverted,' Edward replied coldly as he rose from the table.

Edward had Francis's cynical warning in mind as he dismounted outside the impressive mansion of his employer Thomas Thornhough, Sheriff of Nottinghamshire. It was located in the village of Basford, several miles north of the town boundary. The Thornhough family estate was much further north, near Retford, but Thomas's wealth was such that he could afford to maintain this second home for convenient access to the town where the Shire Hall was situated, in which the most serious criminal business of the county was conducted by royal justices.

It was one of the sheriff's duties to organise the presentments by grand juries that resulted in the trial lists that would be awaiting these justices, and before there could be presentments there had to be investigations and arrests. These were the responsibility of the sheriffs of each county and county borough, and each sheriff relied on their bailiffs to ensure that the gaols were full. There was a presentment day looming for the end of the Michaelmas term, and given that it was now mid-October and the Shire Hall gaol was half empty, Sheriff Thornhough had summoned Edward to explain his apparent slackness.

Edward handed the horse's bridle to the stable groom, then scraped the mud from his boots before announcing his arrival to the steward, who bid him wait in the hallway. With a sinking feeling Edward was advised that he was now authorised to enter the front drawing room, and he had barely done so before the booming voice of the man who paid his stipend confirmed his worst fear.

'In here, Mountsorrel! Stand there and explain to me why, instead of providing the queen's justices with a full calendar for their next assize, you seem to have taken it upon yourself to annoy some of the most important men in both the county and the town.'

'As for the lack of arrests, my lord sheriff,' Edward began in as confident a voice as he could summon, 'there have been few offences of a serious nature of late. The many smaller transgressions have been adequately disposed of by both yourself and the magistrates. It is perhaps a sign of the awe and respect that is due to your office that few have dared commit murder, rape, robbery with arms, sedition, or ought else that would merit an encounter with a queen's justice.'

Thornhough's face set in a grimace as he waved away the excuse. 'I think you miss the point, Mountsorrel. While the absence of miscreants to put before their lordships might be seen by some as a sign of the respect demonstrated towards the law of the realm, others might see it as a failure on my part to fulfil my office — an office that I am destined to vacate in March of next year. If I am to be considered for further office under the Crown, I must be seen to arrest offenders and hold them accountable. Do you understand what I am saying to you?'

'Indeed I do, my lord sheriff. But unless I go out and commit those crimes myself, or wrongfully accuse others of crimes they have not committed, I am at a loss to understand how best to fill the cells below the Shire Hall.'

'Cease your impudence! I have enough examples of that from those who write to me in most unflattering terms regarding your arrogance! These men you have offended are the very same men from whom I will be seeking good opinions when putting my name forward for further office. What explanation do you have for such conduct?'

'Who are those who accuse me of incivility?' Edward asked, though he could have named them without further prompting.

Thornhough reached across his desk and lifted two lengthy pieces of vellum. 'By far the worst comes from Sir Francis Willoughby of Wollaton, who claims to be highly regarded by Her Majesty. He complains that not only did you allow several of his deer to be stolen from under your nose, but you added to your sins by accusing *him* of having stolen them! This is a man who has twice occupied the office that I now hold, and may well be your next employer, unless I dismiss you from my service before then.'

'With the greatest respect to that worthy gentleman,' Edward said, bristling, 'he misunderstood my enquiry of him. True it is that poachers were able to make off with a certain number of his deer herd, but that was solely because we had been misled regarding which part of his vast estate they were to be stolen from. We had advance warning of what was to take place, and it would seem that this warning was deliberately worded so that we were in the wrong area when the crime was committed. I was led to believe, by a town butcher whose word I doubted, that this information had originated from Sir Francis himself.'

'The butcher to whom you refer has also written to complain of your manner,' Thornhough told him as he angrily waved the second vellum. 'He complains that you all but accused him of stealing the venison that he supplied to Sir John Holles — another Nottingham worthy, I might add — on the occasion of his playing host to Robert Cecil on his journey north on the queen's business.'

'Consider it this way,' Edward said. 'It was Alderman Brackenridge who supplied the information that allowed deer to be stolen from the Wollaton estate. When challenged on that point, he claimed to have been so advised by Sir Francis himself, a palpable lie according to Sir Francis. Then the following day, Brackenridge supplied venison to Sir John Holles for a banquet held in honour of Robert Cecil. What conclusions might one reasonably draw?'

'The wrong ones, clearly,' Thornhough insisted. 'I wish to hear no more of the preposterous suggestion that a town alderman would stoop to thieving deer from a respected nobleman and a good friend of his.'

'And if I produce evidence that he did?' Edward asked defiantly.

Thornhough spluttered. 'You will keep it under your bonnet, do you understand me?'

'Yes and no,' Edward replied. 'I understand what you are ordering me to do, but I do not understand why the law may not take its course.'

'There are laws, and then there are laws,' Thornhough insisted. 'The only laws in which I take any interest are those that will consign those accused of serious crime below ground level in the Shire Hall, there to await a trial followed by a hanging. You are to waste no further time in investigating minor matters such as the driving off of deer, do I make myself plain?'

'Indeed you do, my lord sheriff. Might I ask into which category might come the enticing away of young women by lustful and unscrupulous men from London?'

'Do you speak merely of enticement, or perhaps of seizure by force, against their wills?'

'Of that I am not as yet certain,' Edward admitted. 'But I am in the process of making further investigation.'

'Well, it must either be conducted within the next two days or so, or it must be placed in abeyance. I wish you to take as many men as you need by way of *posse comitatus* in order to clear the North Road of any obstruction, and ensure that it is free of cut-throats, vagabonds and others of an evil disposition. It must be clear for passage through to the county border at Bawtry by Friday of this week, when Robert Cecil will be riding north with his party in order to carry messages from Her Majesty to the King of Scotland.'

'He is already biding in Nottingham, of course, as the guest of Sir John Holles,' said Edward. 'Do we know why he is biding here for such a lengthy period?'

'We do not, and neither is it any of our business,' Thornhough replied sharply. 'You would be well advised to follow orders, rather than challenge them. And see to it that you arrest as many as you can creditably accuse of serious crime before the month is out. You are now dismissed from my presence — take care that you are not subsequently dismissed from your office.'

While Edward was quietly cursing his way back into town on horseback, Francis Barton was undergoing a tongue-lashing of a different sort, from the irate cook of Thurland Hall.

'Is that the best you can do?' Rose asked angrily. 'You call yourself the town bailiff, and you can't find one young woman who's gone missing?'

'She may have her own reasons for not wanting to be found,' Francis suggested, making her bristle even more as she waved a heavy pan in the air.

'What are you suggesting?' she demanded. 'That the silly girl's gone off with some man?'

'Is that not possible?' Francis reasoned.

'Of course it's not!' Rose insisted. 'Nell's been brought up to behave like a proper lady, and she knows better than to allow herself to be taken in by some low type who's only interested in getting his hands inside her bodice.'

'So she was happy to stay at home, is that what you're telling me?' Francis fought back as he remembered what he'd been told about Nell's drunken father.

'More likely that than gadding around the town with randy men,' said Rose. 'My Nell's a respectable girl, she is. And you're not going to excuse your failure to find her by pretending that she's anything else, so get out there and look for her.'

'I will once I've looked in your larder,' said Francis.

Rose gave him a scornful look. 'Well, she isn't likely to be in there, is she?'

'All the same...'

'Please yourself, but close the door behind you, to keep the heat out.'

Once inside the capacious larder, Francis headed for the far end, where several sides of meat were hanging from hooks. There was a solitary haunch of venison, and Francis had just noted the blackened and somewhat smeared 'W' brand on its rump when he heard a shout behind him.

'What in God's name are you doing in my larder? Stealing your dinner?'

A red-faced man was standing in the doorway next to a fearful-looking Rose.

'I was instructed to look for venison stolen from the estate of Sir Francis Willoughby,' said Francis.

'Then shouldn't you be bothering the town butchers?' the man demanded.

'No need, since I've found what I was looking for,' Francis replied with satisfaction.

'Your implication, you impudent wretch?'

'The only one possible. Back there is a haunch of venison, which I take to be one left over after the banquet in honour of your exalted guest. Clearly visible on its rump is the letter "W", which is the brand worn by those beasts that graze on the Wollaton estate. I'm prepared at this stage to assume that you were unaware of its origins, but you would be well advised to change your butcher.'

'Do you know who you are addressing with such impudence?'

'Unless I'm mistaken, you're Sir John Holles.'

'You are not mistaken, and you are ordered out of my larder before I run you through as a robber,' Holles threatened him as he reached for his sword hilt.

'Not only am I a skilled swordsman, but I am also bailiff to the Sheriff of Nottingham, William Freeman. The last I heard, it was a capital offence to draw a weapon on an officer of the Crown.'

'Out — now!' Holles screamed.

Francis duly obliged, pausing only to make one final retort as he reached the kitchen doorway. 'I will of course be back, but do not think to hide the evidence, because I have a sound memory. My word will be accepted, even over yours. And no doubt your accomplice Brackenridge will be delighted to give evidence in order to save his own miserable hide.'

5

The din inside The Crusader lessened for a moment as the unruly crowd paused to note who was entering, then reverted to its previous level once it seemed to be no-one of importance. Although Edward was approaching six feet in height, there was nothing about him that made it obvious he was a bailiff, a benefit upon which he regularly traded. Although he was not by any means a regular in this low den, there had been occasions when he'd been obliged to show his face in here. The landlord, Jebediah Tanner, was filling large pots from a barrel and handing them to the young woman at the counter. He scowled as Edward pushed his way through the eagerly waiting throng and raised his voice to be heard above the clamour.

'I'm Edward Mountsorrel, bailiff to the county sheriff, and I'm making enquiries regarding the whereabouts of a young lady called Nell Franklin.'

'Tell him nothing,' Tanner growled as he handed up another filled pot, which the young woman placed on the counter in front of her. 'He's nothing but trouble, so keep it shut.'

'What did she look like?' the young woman asked.

Edward repeated the description of Nell that he'd been given by her mother. The young woman's eyes seemed to flicker in recognition as she nevertheless shook her head.

Tanner stood back upright and approached the counter. 'Plenty of prostitutes come in here, but we don't encourage them. If they want to make a private arrangement with one of the customers, that's their business, of course, but we don't allow them in here on their own.'

'She wouldn't have been here alone, from what I was told,' Edward persevered. 'My information is that she was in here with a man named Richard, and that they had a regular relationship.'

'Like I said,' said Tanner, 'if they are with a man, that's fair enough, and we don't enquire as to their business, but they don't get to come in here on their own, so get lost. The front door's just behind you.'

Edward ignored him and gave the young woman his best smile. 'What's your name?' he asked with an admiring look.

The young woman made a pretence of lowering her gaze in modesty, despite the fact that her duties no doubt exposed her to lascivious looks, disgusting invitations and wandering hands on a daily basis. 'I'm Ellie — short for Eleanor.'

'Well, Ellie, it seems to me that if I were wishing to entertain a comely young lady like yourself in here, I'd find it rather restricting with all this noise and constant coming and going. There appear to be no seats in this part of the establishment, so if I wanted to invite you to take a drink with me, where would we go?'

'You've not got time to dally with this troublemaker,' Tanner told her gruffly. 'Get those pots lined up, and start collecting the customers' money.'

As fast as the pots appeared on the top of the counter, eager hands were reaching out to claim them. Ellie took their coins and dropped them into the pot on the shelf just below the counter. As Edward stood politely waiting to regain her full attention, she looked briefly behind her, then jerked her head to indicate a passageway down the left-hand side of the counter, as viewed from Edward's perspective. He mouthed a silent thanks and made his way into the passageway, down one side of which were small enclaves with benches and tables.

They were built in such a way that the occupants of each enclave would be unable to see anyone in the other enclaves.

Several of the booths were occupied, and each contained a man and a furtive-looking woman who was almost certainly a local prostitute. Edward was forced to look away in embarrassment on several occasions when he saw what they were doing, and he earned himself more than one surly oath.

He stopped at every enclave and asked the women within if they'd seen Nell Franklin recently, but they all shook their heads and gave him looks of annoyance. He came to the last enclave, which appeared to be empty until he noticed something lying under the table. It was a neck scarf, red with white emblems that resembled castles, and he picked it up and put it to his nose in case it retained traces of a lady's perfume. When it turned out to smell more like a stable, he screwed it up and stuffed it into his doublet pocket, then looked back up towards the entrance to the main taproom, from where Tanner was glaring at him.

'There's nothing down there of any interest to you, and I've warned you more than once to leave the premises. I know the law as well as you do, and bailiff or not I'd be entitled to have you thrown out, since you've got no lawful business in here. You've made your enquiries about the woman and got nowhere, so leave. Now.'

'Your willing co-operation has been duly noted, and will be relayed in due course to the magistrates,' Edward said as he brushed past the landlord and heaved his way through the noisy taproom. He emerged into the Rockyard, as the lane that led back round the base of the castle rock was known. Over to his right the River Leen oozed along to the south of Nottingham.

He heard a faint call from behind him and turned to see Ellie hurrying towards him. She pulled him into the shade of an overhanging house gable so that they could not be seen by anyone leaving The Crusader.

'That young woman you were asking about,' she whispered. 'She was in the place a few nights ago, but she wasn't the only one.'

'Your meaning?'

'That man you were also asking about — named Richard? He's been in the place almost every night for a week or so now, with a different woman each time. Then we never see any more of the woman he's been entertaining.'

'So he has a lusty nature, and prefers a different woman every night,' Edward offered by way of explanation.

Ellie shook her head. 'No, it's worse than that. Two of the women were regulars in here, and one of them — Jane Ballander — was a friend of mine. I haven't seen her since she told me she was going to London with Richard, but the next night he was with another woman who sounds a lot like the one you're looking for. I haven't seen Jane since. Same with the other woman — she's called of Mary, but I don't know her last name. She never missed a day in The Crusader, and she did well out of what she got up to in the room upstairs, but on the night she was with Richard, she never come back into the taproom.'

'So she was in one of those enclaves with this man calling himself Richard, but never came out again — is that what you're telling me?' Edward asked in disbelief.

Ellie nodded. 'There's something else you should know,' she told him with a fearful look as she lowered her voice. 'At the end of that passageway with the little enclaves in it, there's a door.'

'Where does it lead?'

'No idea, because I've never been allowed behind it. It's hidden behind what's made to look like a cupboard, but the landlord says to ignore it. If anybody asks, we're to say that we never knew it were there.'

'This man, Richard — can you describe him?' Edward asked, anxious that their interview might be coming to an end.

'I don't need to — you've already seen him,' said Ellie. 'He was the one with the green bonnet who was in the second enclave from the end, sitting with the woman who had red hair.'

Edward had a vague memory of the couple in question, and he thanked Ellie for her assistance. 'I'll probably come back in the next day or so with a colleague — if I do, could you point out this Richard for me?'

'If it'll help to find Jane, though I'll probably be out of a job. Still, there are plenty of other alehouses where they can use a young woman with quick hands. Now, I've got to go back.'

Back at home, Edward found Francis in the rear garden, discussing with Dickon what he might cook for supper after he'd finished beating his bed bolster. Dickon's sleeping quarters were at the rear of the kitchen, where he spent most of his day when not cleaning out the main house.

'How went matters at Thurland Hall?' Edward asked.

Francis grinned. 'I found a haunch of venison with the Wollaton brand mark on it, so there can be no doubt where the stolen deer ended up.'

'We cannot be sure that the poachers were stealing to order for Sir John Holles, though, can we?'

Francis shook his head. 'Sir John said as much when he ordered me out of his grand residence. But since we are almost certain that we can prove the deer to have been supplied by Brackenridge, we can surely report him?'

Edward shrugged. 'He will simply claim that when approached by those in possession of the venison, he had no idea where it had come from.'

'A likely story! There are very few deer herds so close to the town, and the carcasses would have clearly displayed their brands. Whether or not Brackenridge knew that particular brand to be that of Sir Francis Willoughby, the very existence of the brands should have alerted him to the fact that they had come from a private collection, and had not been taken in the wild.'

'Is this the same man who so recently advised me that it was unwise to proceed against those who are well connected?' asked Edward, smiling. 'I certainly had that point reinforced earlier today, when my sheriff all but promised to dismiss me if I made any accusation against either Brackenridge or Holles. I've been left in no doubt that I shall be seeking further employment should I further displease any of those whom Thornhough will be seeking to appease in order to acquire high office when his term as sheriff ends.'

'The same will no doubt be true of Sheriff Freeman, here in the town,' Francis confirmed gloomily. 'Added to all this was the angry response I got from Rose Franklin when I told her that we had found no trace of her daughter.'

'There is more news to impart on that matter, but none that will bring any comfort to Mistress Franklin,' said Edward. 'I fear that The Crusader is being used as a place from which to abduct young women of the loose sort.'

'Why would anyone need to abduct a doxy in order to have their way with them, when they can simply pay?' Francis argued.

'Some brutes prefer to take it forcefully. Whatever the reason, I fear that more women have been spirited away, and it's unlikely that Nottingham will see them again. Not alive, anyway.'

'And how many do you think may have been taken?' Francis asked as they walked back towards the house.

Edward counted them on his fingers as they walked. 'We know Nell Franklin to be missing. You also mentioned another young woman called Annie, did you not?'

'Annie Freebourne, yes. Are there more?'

'So I was told by a young woman called Ellie who sells pots at The Crusader. She named two more — Jane Ballander, who was a particular friend of hers, and another woman called Mary. That makes four altogether, by my count. And they were all last seen in the company of a man named Richard.'

'That was the name I was given by the women in The Dog and Partridge when I first made enquiry regarding Nell Franklin!' Francis shouted excitedly. 'Could the same man be associated with the other three women?'

'So I believe,' Edward confirmed. 'According to Ellie, each of the women was occupying a private table there with a man called Richard when they were last seen. You should know that off to the left of the taproom counter is a passageway that is fitted out with small enclaves. You can only see what's going on in any of them by standing out in the passageway itself. From what I saw today, one can take a great many liberties with a lady while in one of those enclaves. At the end of the passageway is a door that the landlord, Tanner, forbids the staff to go through. It's obscured by a cupboard, and I suspect that the women are being overpowered, perhaps drugged, then slipped out through that doorway to a dreadful fate.'

By this time, the bailiffs had taken a seat at the table in their main room and were waiting for Dickon to serve their supper.

'We must investigate what is behind this cupboard,' Francis said after a short silence.

'Indeed we must, but what evidence do we have to justify such an intrusion?'

'If Ellie can testify as to the existence of this hidden door,' Francis suggested, 'then we can claim that we believe it to be hiding Catholic priests.'

'Catholic priests in an alehouse?' Edward laughed. 'How likely is that?'

'They've been discovered everywhere else, or so I've heard,' Francis insisted, 'and Her Majesty has put a bounty on their heads. I've heard of them being found in chimneys, behind false wall panels, in cellars, down wells and even inside outdoor middens. Queen Elizabeth has a morbid fear that they are being used to foment rebellion, and she would not only authorise what we are proposing, but would applaud it. We might even have approached Robert Cecil for his leave to do it, but he is no doubt long departed.'

'That's something else,' said Edward. 'I have been commanded by Sheriff Thornhough to clear the North Road of vagrants, cut-purses and other undesirables all the way to Bawtry, for Cecil's onward progress on Friday.'

'Isn't that part of your duties?'

'Of course, but ask yourself why Robert Cecil would be biding in Nottingham for so long. If, as is put abroad, he is on urgent business for Her Majesty, then surely he would not wish to delay that business for longer than is necessary.'

'It's none of our business,' Francis argued, 'and the good Lord knows we have enough to do without concerning ourselves about how long Cecil bides in the town, enjoying stolen venison.'

'It just seems odd.'

'There is much that is odd in those matters we are called to deal with, Edward. Now, unless my stomach is sending fantasies to my eyes, here comes Dickon with our supper. I for one will be pleased to forget all about venison for a brief while, and let us pray that this roast fowl did not come from Master Brackenridge's establishment.'

6

In the middle of the night Edward woke sharply, coughing and choking. He shot to his feet and staggered to the second bedchamber, where he shook Francis awake.

'Francis, move! We're on fire!'

They weaved their way down the stairs and out into the rear garden, just as the back wall of their house collapsed onto the grass behind them. Ahead of them was the kitchen, almost razed to the ground, and a stiff wind was still driving sparks towards the house. It was clear that the conflagration must have begun in the kitchen.

Both men immediately feared for Dickon's safety. They undertook a rapid search through the smouldering embers of the kitchen, only to find his remains. The fire hadn't killed him, although it had burned his body severely; the cause of his death was a large knife firmly embedded in his ribs.

'Bastards!' Edward yelled. 'Dirty, cowardly bastards! This fire was meant for us, but they didn't shrink from killing poor Dickon in the process! I'll run through the villain who did this, once I discover who he is — and I won't cease until I do!'

Francis took a deep breath and held his nose with one hand, while extracting the knife with the other. 'You may not have to look far. This type of knife belongs only to the likes of a butcher.'

'Brackenridge!'

'Either he, or someone working on his orders. Dickon was clearly murdered so that the swine could burn us where we slept. We must be closer to proving that he poached the deer than we thought.'

'Why would anyone seek to murder two bailiffs simply to cover up their involvement in a crime that, given Brackenridge's connections, would probably result in little more than a fine?' Edward demanded.

'The man seeks to be Mayor of Nottingham, does he not? *Any* appearance in a court would severely hamper that ambition.'

'Perhaps it was not that matter at all,' Edward suggested. 'The only other man whose feathers I've ruffled recently, and who would be capable of such a low act, is that rat Tanner, who owns The Crusader. Perhaps he sought to stop me from looking behind his cupboard.'

Francis looked behind him and groaned. 'Whatever the reason, and whoever the culprit, these are matters we may consider only when we have somewhere else to live.'

Edward also turned back to gaze hopelessly at the inferno, just as a side wall collapsed, taking the entire upper floor with it as it crashed to the ground. Neighbours had been alerted by the roar of the flames and the bright light, and they stood in the lane, watching the blaze. None of them was making any effort to douse the flames, since the property sat on a plot of land that was wide enough to ensure that none of the neighbouring houses were at risk, and the wind was sending the embers towards a portion of empty land across the lane.

By the time the sun had risen, Edward and Francis had laid Dickon's remains out on the rear lawn in as respectful a fashion as was possible. They then wandered back into the blackened remains of their former residence to search for anything they might salvage. Their swords had survived the inferno, as had a few metal pots, but otherwise they were destitute.

However, they were soon reminded of the respect with which Francis in particular was regarded by the law-abiding members of the town he served. Within the first hour after dawn, townspeople began arriving with spare clothing, jugs of ale and loaves of bread. Mistress Broadwood from three houses up the street invited them into her home to get warm and help themselves to as much potage as they could consume. Some months ago, Francis had dived behind her stall at the Saturday market to prevent two ruffians making off with her woven baskets. Before Edward and Francis had finished eating, three more grateful fellow townsmen had arrived with clothing more appropriate for their public office, while a local lad had been down to the stables in the neighbouring street where the bailiffs kept their horses. He tied them to the fence posts outside the Broadwood house after assuring both men that their mounts had come to no harm, and he thanked Francis yet again for not reporting his theft of apples from the churchyard of St Nicholas's.

'You are clearly highly regarded,' said Edward as he finished washing the soot from his face using the bowl of water provided by a smiling Anne Broadwood.

'Not so highly regarded, I think, that anyone would wish to grant us a permanent presence in their house,' said Francis. 'We must find somewhere new to live until our own house can be rebuilt. We must also see to a decent Christian burial for Dickon.'

'As to the latter,' Edward replied, 'he once told me that he came from farming stock in Kinoulton, a village to the south of here. I'll alert the minister of St Nicholas's to the need for a funeral, and send word to the Squire of Kinoulton that a lad called Dickon has been slain by an evil hand. Do you know if he had a second name?'

'No, but he once told me that he had a sister in the town here, married to a fuller who resides in Wheelwright Lane. I'll have word sent there also. Now, what about a temporary residence for ourselves?'

'I've been giving that some thought, while filling my grateful stomach with this excellent potage,' said Edward. 'It put me in mind of the food we were constantly being fed when I served under the Earl of Leicester, which led me to thoughts of my days as a soldier. This reminded me of where we might seek charity.'

'Did you intend to share this wondrous revelation with me, or must I seek a bed in an orphanage?'

'No,' Edward replied, 'you need only walk down to the bottom of this street.'

Francis thought for a moment, then his jaw dropped. 'You allude to the castle?'

'And why not? We are both ultimately servants of the queen whose castle it is, and we may, I believe, throw ourselves upon the mercy of its constable.'

'If you so advise, but you should know that I have not enjoyed the best of relationships with the colonel of the garrison there, given the frequency with which I have been obliged to lay criminal charges against the ruffians who pass for his men.'

'Then leave me to do the talking,' Edward replied, 'given that the castle is rightly within the county anyway.'

Less than an hour later, dressed in the finest raiment that had been bestowed upon them by their charitable neighbours, the bailiffs trotted their horses up the slope to the gatehouse that dominated the castle's southern wall, only a few feet above the roadway. A sentry with a ceremonial halberd, but with a very useable sword hanging from his belt, demanded to know their business.

'I am Edward Mountsorrel, bailiff to the Sheriff of Nottinghamshire, in which capacity I seek audience with the castle constable,' Edward announced.

They were instructed to wait while a messenger was dispatched to the collection of dilapidated buildings that lay further up the slope. There was a lengthy delay, during which a light snowfall obliged them to seek permission to sit on horseback under the gatehouse archway. Finally a tall, portly gentleman rode down the slope on a horse of his own, accompanied by two armed guards carrying pikes in addition to their swords. The man dismounted and walked under the archway, causing Edward and Francis to also dismount in a silent gesture of respect.

'Which of you is from the county sheriff's office?' the man demanded, having identified himself as the castellan.

Edward gave a small bow. 'I am he. Edward Mountsorrel.'

'And this other man is your servant?' the man asked haughtily.

'I am Bailiff Barton, from the office of the Sheriff of Nottingham,' Francis replied sharply.

Their inquisitor's face showed his displeasure. 'The oaf who continually has the men of my garrison locked up on spurious charges?'

'No, the man who protects the innocent townsfolk of Nottingham from the depredations of those wretches who pass themselves off as soldiers. You clearly recall who I am, given that we have met more than once in recent times, so do not insult me further.'

'What is your business here?' the man demanded of Edward, having half turned his back on Francis in a gesture of disdain.

Edward decided that it would be politic for at least one of them to retain the man's good opinion, so he kept his manner polite. 'We are obliged to prevail upon your charity in order to have a roof over our heads for the foreseeable future. Our own domicile was burned down around us by those who seek to obstruct certain enquiries we are in the process of conducting.'

'What enquiries might those be?'

'We could only confide their details to the castle constable, given his position of authority under the Crown.'

'You will be waiting a long time to speak to the constable, unless you are prepared to hover by his kitchen door at Belvoir Castle, half a day's ride to the south. The title of constable is devolved from one generation to the next, along with the title of the Earl of Rutland. The family hold the title in perpetuity, but they take their duties lightly except when royalty is in attendance — which given the lamentable state of this place is never. Even the queen's emissaries prefer to lodge in the town proper.'

'Just as Master Cecil currently abides at Thurland Hall?' Francis interjected.

The colonel ignored him. 'I am Thomas Waldegrave, Colonel in Chief of the Castle Garrison,' he said. 'I am responsible for maintaining military discipline as well as ensuring that what is left of the noble pile behind me remains as intact as nature will allow. It is a ruin with a splendid history, once beloved of the monarchs of England when they rode to the hunt in the forests to the north of the town. But it is in a poor state, with barely enough accommodation for the hundred or so souls who eke out a thoroughly resented term of duty, performing tasks that become increasingly irrelevant to the safety of the realm. Not even I regard my current posting as anything worthy of celebration. But, such as it is, you are welcome to our hospitality. You may disclose to me what has led to someone attempting to burn you alive.'

'We thank you most heartily,' Edward replied, not yet wishing to talk about the investigation. 'I shall see to it that Sheriff Thornhough is duly apprised of your civility and assistance. To where should we now proceed?'

'You will find space in the officers' quarters of the barracks behind us,' Waldegrave told them, waving his hand towards the ruins up the hill. 'Pray accompany me, and I will give instruction that you are to be treated as befits your office.'

As Edward and Francis walked their mounts up the steep slope that led to their temporary accommodation, they saw half a dozen men at arms being drilled on the flat area of ground immediately in front of the main entrance to the barracks. Edward's eyebrows rose as they got closer and he took in what they were wearing, and he turned to address Waldegrave.

'That is a fine livery. Particularly the tunic fronts, which sport a splendid design. Was it of your own devising?'

'Indeed it was,' Waldegrave said proudly. 'I cannot recall what heraldic description was applied to it, but as you can see it is a field of scarlet on which are picked out castles in white, to depict the place that the men are sworn to defend.'

They soon arrived at the barracks, and Edward and Francis were shown to the narrow room that they would be sharing.

'What was all that nonsense about the tunics that the men were wearing?' Francis demanded as they threw what few possessions they still had onto their hard bolsters. 'Was it merely part of your rather overdone attempt to keep in with that inflated pig's bladder of a colonel?'

'Yes and no,' said Edward, 'but if we are to enjoy a modicum of comfort in this draughty old hovel — and in particular if we are to avoid being poisoned or run through — then it will be as well to humour him. As it is, I learned something of considerable interest.'

'What, precisely?' Francis asked.

Edward lowered his voice. 'Remember how I told you of those enclaves down the side passageway in The Crusader? The place in which four women that we know of — and possibly more — were entertained by the man calling himself Richard? Well, on the floor under the table in the end enclave — the one closest to the cupboard that hides a secret door — I found a piece of cloth that I took to be a lady's scarf or suchlike, until I was unwise enough to put it to my nose. It smelt like a stable, and it bore the same design as that on the soldiers' uniforms: a red background with white castles picked out at regular intervals. It occurs to me that it may have been a piece from a tunic, or more likely a saddlecloth, and could have been used to bind a woman's wrists.'

'So you suspect someone from the castle guard of having been involved in the disappearance of those women?'

'Don't you agree, in the circumstances?'

'Quite possibly. Do you still have this cloth?'

Edward shook his head. 'Regrettably it was lost in the fire. But we cannot ignore what it signified. We must obviously remain silent about it while we are here.'

'I noticed that you avoided advising our host of our investigation,' Francis observed.

Edward nodded. 'Some sixth sense urged me to silence, and now I have been vindicated. Should we receive any more enquiries, say only that we are seeking those who stole deer from Wollaton Hall. Which reminds me — what day is this?'

'It is Tuesday.'

'Then tomorrow I have an invitation to return to Wollaton.'

'I was under the impression that Sir Francis had ordered you off his estate,' said Francis.

'So he did, but my invitation comes from a delightful young lady whose better acquaintance I would dearly love to cultivate. If anyone asks, I will be making further enquiries into the missing deer.'

Later that day, Edward and Francis stood on what was left of the castle's east terrace, gazing at the view of the old town. The spire of St Mary's Church was the most obvious landmark.

'We thought we might take a turn round your battlements before supper,' Edward offered by way of explanation as Colonel Waldegrave walked towards them.

'Don't venture too near the edge,' Waldegrave told them. 'We lose lumps of it every time there's a heavy frost followed by a thaw.'

'Thank you for the warning,' Francis muttered as he stepped smartly backwards, although the expression on Waldegrave's face suggested that he regretted having given it.

The colonel turned to Edward. 'You never did get around to telling me what led to someone burning down your house.'

Edward allowed his face to fall as he supplied the half-truth. 'We were investigating the theft of several deer from the Wollaton estate, which belongs to Sir Francis Willoughby. I'd all but established that it had found its way into Thurston Hall, whose owner is currently entertaining Master Robert Cecil as he breaks his journey north on Her Majesty's business.'

'I am well aware of that,' Waldegrave nodded, 'since his escort have been billeted here ever since he arrived. Master Cecil may well be enjoying the finest hospitality, but those who accompany him are required to endure far less gracious surroundings. You will meet them at supper, of course, and I may also advise you that I have been asked to supplement Cecil's escort with twenty of my own men as they continue north next Friday. But surely you do not suspect Sir John Holles of being party to the poaching of deer?'

'Indeed not,' Edward agreed readily. 'But we *do* have grounds for suspecting the merchant who supplied the venison. A man called Henry Brackenridge.'

'*Alderman* Brackenridge,' Francis added. 'Presumably you are about to advise us of what a fine upstanding citizen he is?'

Waldegrave gave him a look of disdain, then shook his head. 'I cannot comment on anything except the quality of his meat, which has more than once poisoned my men. It is to be hoped that his venison was of a better quality, or he may face the Tower for seeking to do away with a Cecil.'

'What was that?' Francis asked in response to a dismal wail that seemed to float around them.

'What?' Waldegrave asked hastily.

The cry was repeated, and this time all three men heard it. '*That*,' Francis said as he and Edward looked nervously towards Waldegrave.

For a moment the colonel seemed at a loss to explain, but he quickly regained his composure. 'You have been treated to a rare privilege granted to few, gentlemen. You have just heard the ghosts of the Welsh boys.'

'They sounded more like live women,' Francis argued.

Waldegrave shook his head. 'Would that they were, and that the curse had been lifted.' He paused for dramatic effect. 'This castle was once a favoured watering hole of King John, several centuries ago. He was constantly at war with the Welsh, and after yet another peace treaty that he had no confidence that the Welsh would keep, he brought almost thirty young Welsh boys of royal blood back here as hostages. Then when the treacherous brigands rose up against him again, he ordered that these helpless boys be brought out and hanged from these very battlements. Their wails and pleas for mercy were said to be dreadful to hear, and from time to time we are reminded of the foul deed by their ghostly repetitions. It is said that they can only be heard by honourable men. Regard yourselves as highly regarded by the wraiths of the departed, gentlemen, and now let us away to our supper.'

As the bailiffs prepared for bed later that evening, Francis brought up Waldegrave's story. 'Did you believe that pigswill about the ghosts of Welsh boys?' he asked.

'No more than you did, by the look on your face,' said Edward. 'But you were correct in believing, as did I, that they sounded more like the anguished cries of young women. Would that we had the authority to have this dreadful place searched! I believe that the answer to our quest for the missing women lies somewhere within these walls. You might wish to investigate as much of this Godforsaken place as you can on the morrow, while I take care of more pleasurable business at Wollaton.'

7

Edward stepped out from behind an oak trunk, smiling broadly. Elizabeth returned his smile as she quickened her steps down the rose garden and took his arm. Then she cast an anxious eye back in the direction from which she had just come.

'You are both eager and bold, Master Mountsorrel, but do you not fear that your presence will be noted, and the dogs set upon you? The master is most protective of his estate, and it was the talk of the kitchen that you had been ordered never to return here.'

'Nothing could deter me from renewing our acquaintance,' Edward replied with a gracious half bow. 'As for being detected, you forget that I was once a soldier, and we are trained to hide and creep up on the enemy.'

'Be that as it may, you are surely exposed to view as you walk with me?'

'While we are in the rose garden, certainly,' Edward agreed, 'but as I recall, there is a wooded walk to the left where we may talk unobserved.'

'Your memory is excellent.'

'I remember every single moment of that joyous time spent in your company,' Edward said gallantly as they turned to their left. 'And now, as I also recall, you will be obliged to retain my arm as we step over these dividing stones. Hopefully it will remain there for some time after that.'

'You have a courteous manner, for one who was raised as an orphan,' Elizabeth replied. She tightened her grip on his arm as they stepped into the long walk, and she did not let go as they began to move down the path. Halfway along there was a rustic bench that Edward suggested they sit on.

As they sat gazing at the ten-foot high bush on the other side of the walk, Edward broke the silence.

'I am surely not the only one at risk, should we be seen together. Would your master not be aggrieved to learn that you agreed to walk with me, knowing that he has made it clear that I am not welcome on his estate? You were there when he bade me depart and not return, were you not?'

'Indeed I was, but could I be held to account for simply acting civilly when you appeared halfway through my weekly walk, and gallantly offered to accompany me?'

Edward chuckled. 'Clearly you are a lady of sharp wits and an independent spirit. Do you make such excuses every time that you allow yourself to be accompanied by a man on your weekly walk?'

Elizabeth snorted. 'Do not insult my intelligence, Master Mountsorrel.'

'My name is Edward, mistress. Please feel free to employ it, as I was invited to call you Elizabeth.'

'Whatever your name may be, do not presume that I am naive,' she replied stiffly, looking him in the eye. 'Your question was clearly designed to discover whether or not I enjoy the company of other men when my duties permit. Why not ask me directly?'

'Very well,' Edward replied with a twinkle in his eye. 'Mistress Porter — Elizabeth — do you have a regular companion when you take your weekly walk through the gardens of your employer's estate?'

'If I did, I would hardly have invited you to join me today, would I? No, Edward, I have no regular male companion when I take my weekly walk.'

'Would you accept me as your regular companion on your walk through these exquisite gardens every Wednesday after dinner?'

'I would be happy to do so. Now, let us abandon the pretence. We are both, I suspect, lonely people, each of us for a different reason. For you it is the lack of parents or siblings, and your memories of the cold charity of an orphanage.'

'And for you?'

'The need to maintain an aloof dignity, and behave as befits a lady of breeding, in order to attract a husband. But I did not always behave as my parents would have wished. Had I done so, I would now be married to a steward, a head footman, or —God forbid — a tradesman from a nearby town. As matters stand, I am a free woman.'

'A free woman who is nevertheless obliged to serve others for her livelihood.'

'Not forever, I hope. But I must own that my current duties keep me closely confined to my mistress's side, so that marriage sometimes seems a long way off.'

'You do not get to meet many eligible young men, you mean?' Edward asked.

'I do not. My master is most desirous of elevation at court, and his greatest wish is for Her Majesty to pay us a visit here at Wollaton. To this end, he never overlooks any opportunity to ingratiate himself with those of her court who are known to be in favour. Only last week we received a brief visit from Robert Cecil, whose father was until recently the queen's closest adviser. The conversation during the tedious banquet that we were all obliged to attend — myself standing respectfully to the side for nearly four hours — was all about who was in favour at court, who was in rivalry with who, and so much tittle-tattle of that ilk that I wanted to fall asleep. And next week we shall have to endure it again, when we play host to the man whom Cecil boldly declared to be his greatest rival for the queen's ear — the Earl of Essex. That, of course, affects you in two ways.'

'How so?' Edward asked, intrigued. 'I am of course aware that Robert Cecil has been staying in the town on his journey north on the queen's business, since I am charged with the duty of clearing the road of undesirables ahead of his progress. But what do you mean regarding the Earl of Essex?'

'You really do not know who he is? You told me you served in the army of the Earl of Leicester.'

'I did. In the great camp at Tilbury, where we lay in wait for the Spanish.'

'Was the Earl of Essex not there also?'

'Not that I recall — why should he have been?'

'Because he is the stepson of the late Earl of Leicester, or so it is said. They tell of Robert Dudley having married the earl's mother, to the queen's great disapproval. So that makes Essex the stepson of your great hero and patron.'

'How do you know he was my patron?' Edward asked sharply.

Elizabeth blushed. 'You must forgive me, but I overheard a conversation that perhaps I should not have. You may not be aware, but the master sent a letter of complaint to your employer following the loss of the deer from the park.'

'Believe me, I was well aware of that,' Edward said, frowning.

'Well, your employer called at the house and was received in the drawing room by the master, who instructed that I remove therefrom certain needlepoint items that my mistress had been working on. As I did so, I became aware that they were discussing you. Since we had recently become acquainted, I took my time in removing the items, and thereafter kept listening from the far side of the door, which I left ajar. Was that a wicked thing to do?'

'Not if you can tell me what was said about me,' Edward replied, grinning conspiratorially.

Elizabeth needed no further encouragement. 'Well, your employer advised the master that you had become his bailiff on the personal recommendation of the Earl of Leicester, and that in his opinion there was no man more loyal or efficient than you.'

Edward laughed as he recalled what Thornhough had said to him face to face. 'Those were not quite the glowing endearments that he bestowed upon me while lamenting my failure to apprehend the poachers.'

'Be that as it may, such was the way in which he described you. I noted your preferment by such a leading noble who, it was rumoured, was the queen's favourite.'

'Whether he was or not, he died shortly afterwards, more's the pity. So that is one way in which the impending visit of his stepson Essex might be of passing interest to me. What, pray, is the second?'

'He is due here next Tuesday. There is to be another interminable banquet on the following day, which will mean that we cannot enjoy another meeting a week today.'

'Will you not be allowed another brief release from your duties on another day, to compensate?'

'Perhaps, but I do not know when. It is only because my mistress is in the habit of taking to her bedchamber on Wednesday afternoons — for what she calls "a period of restorative sleep" — that I am able to make any plans at all. Since she is invariably accompanied by her husband, it is said throughout the house that her withdrawal is for carnal purposes, since they normally occupy separate rooms in the west wing.'

Edward blushed. 'We should perhaps speak no more of that. Tell me, rather, what it is that has made the Earl of Essex the enemy of Robert Cecil.'

'I did not say that they were enemies. The word Master Cecil employed was "rivals", and it was in the context of having the queen's ear. It would seem that Cecil is in favour of maintaining cordial relations with the Scots, despite the mischief wrought by their late queen, while Essex is forever offering to take a force north to enforce what he calls "our national interests". I take this to mean putting Edinburgh to the torch in retaliation for their former queen's threat to Her Majesty's throne.'

Edward gazed back at her in admiration. 'You are knowledgeable regarding matters of politics and national affairs.'

'It is all I hear discussed when I stand silently behind my mistress at family mealtimes. I watch them consuming vast quantities of venison, wood pigeon and capons while we in the servants' kitchen are forced to make do with cabbage broth and black bread. And speaking of the kitchen, here comes one of those who labour in it. Fear not, she can be trusted.'

While she had been speaking, a slip of a girl in a plain grey smock had been running, barefoot, down the path from the side entrance to the main house, which gave access to the servants' quarters. She came to a halt and doubled over to catch her breath, allowing Elizabeth to effect the introductions.

'This is Amy from the kitchen, a biddable girl who looks after my interests in the hope that I can secure her a maid's job in the main house. She promised to alert me should my presence be required. What is it, Amy? Has my mistress arisen from her slumbers earlier than she is wont to do?'

'No, begging your pardon and all. It's this gentleman I seek, if he is Bailiff Mountsorrel.' Amy turned to Edward. 'There is a man looking for you. He currently sits by the kitchen door in a great deal of sweat, with a horse that looks fit to die. I hope we shan't be called upon to eat it for dinner if it does.'

'There is a man at the kitchen door who asks for me?' Edward asked as he rose hastily to his feet. 'Does your master therefore know that I am here?'

'No, sir, begging your pardon and all. The master's away at his coalmine in the village. But the man at the kitchen door says to tell you that you need to go back into town urgently. He wouldn't say why.'

Edward turned back to Elizabeth with a helpless shrug. 'It would seem that my duties, like yours, must take priority. I know not when we might meet again, but hopefully it will be soon. In the meantime … well…'

Elizabeth rose from the bench with a smile, took his hand and kissed him on the cheek. 'If we are destined to meet again, then we shall. I certainly hope that to be the case. Do not concern yourself regarding Amy — she is very good at feigning failing eyesight when the occasion demands.'

'Lead me to this man,' Edward said to Amy, savouring the lingering sensation of Elizabeth's kiss. They scurried through a side entrance, down several internal corridors and through the kitchen, where the cook shouted at them to take care. They then emerged into the open air once more, where a white-faced man sat with his back to the kitchen wall. He looked up as Edward appeared.

'Bailiff Mountsorrel?'

'The very same.'

'I'm Caleb Muncey. I serve Bailiff Barton when he has need of men. He now has need of you: a body has been pulled out of the Leen down in the east croft.'

Edward retrieved his horse from where he'd hidden it, tied to one of the beech trees in the copse alongside the herd-master's hut, and rode down the long slope that led to the Derby Road gate. He then swung left to head back into town as fast as the horse could go.

Less than an hour later he breasted Turncalf Bridge and looked to his left, down into the easternmost of the two crofts that constituted the area known as the Meadows, south of the town proper, which lay between the rivers Leen and Trent. A small crowd had assembled on the south bank of the Leen that he had just crossed, and the tall figure of Francis Barton, with his bald patch glistening in the wintry sun between his remaining ginger tufts, stood out above the rest. Francis looked up as he heard the approaching hooves, and walked over as Edward hastily dismounted.

'My apologies for interrupting your tryst, Edward, but I thought you'd better be consulted on this, since there's some doubt over which of us has jurisdiction.'

He had a valid point. The Meadows lay to the south of Narrow Marsh, the cramped slum area that was at the southern perimeter of the town. As a result, the east and west crofts that made up the Meadows lay geographically beyond the boundaries of the jurisdiction of the town bailiff. However, since those with trading rights regularly ran their beasts over its rich marsh grasses, while people from the pestilential lanes of Narrow Marsh sought fresh air by walking through the Meadows down to the banks of the Trent, it was popularly regarded as being part of the town proper. There was normally no problem with this curious duality, since Francis cheerfully supervised the work of those constables who were sent into the Meadows to retrieve fallen drunks, rescue young women from their would-be violators, and ensure that cattle were not driven off under the cover of darkness.

However, it was a different consideration when the crime was a serious matter that would be tried in the Assize Court, ahead of which rival sheriffs would compete for the privilege of presenting the culprit. There was also the desire on Francis's part not to have any further source of conflict with Edward. He walked him over to where a sad and soggy bundle lay on the riverbank, awaiting his attention.

'She was pulled out by that man over there, who was walking his dog along the bank and saw what he took to be a bundle of clothing tied to an overhanging tree branch,' Francis told him. 'As you can see, it turned out to be a young woman, and by my calculation she must have drifted downstream until she got caught by the branch. So perhaps there can be no argument, and the matter comes within your remit.'

Edward rolled the body over with his boot, then gave a gasp of surprise and recognition. There could be little doubt that the woman had been murdered, since the yawning gap in her throat was wide enough to reveal the bone beneath.

'You surmised correctly, Francis,' said Edward. 'Her name was Ellie, short for Eleanor, and she served pots in The Crusader.'

'So may we conclude that she was killed somewhere near The Crusader?' Francis asked.

'Either that or *in* it,' Edward said with a grimace. 'It was she who told me of the goings-on in those enclaves in there, and the disappearance of women who had recently made the acquaintance of the man called Richard. God help her, she must have been seen or overheard talking to me by whoever slit her throat. It seems that the activities in The Crusader are even more serious than we first thought.'

'So her employer may have arranged for her to be silenced?'

'By the look of him, Jeb Tanner is more than capable of doing such a thing himself,' Edward snarled as he spat into the grass. 'I suggest that we pay him a visit.'

'Is it your matter or mine?' Francis asked doubtfully.

Edward glared angrily along the bank of the Leen. 'If my suspicions are correct, then it's a county matter, since the poor woman was murdered at The Crusader, which lies outside the town. But this part of the Meadows is popularly regarded as lying within the curtilage of Nottingham, so that makes it yours. More to the point, I suggest, any witnesses to the foul deed will be from the town, and will therefore seek to contact you in the Guildhall.'

Having made arrangements for the body to be taken up to the outhouse at the rear of the Guildhall, Edward and Francis strode swiftly to The Crusader, whose taproom was bursting with customers. The bailiffs pushed their way through the throng to the counter, where a middle-aged woman was exchanging pots for pennies. Behind her, Jeb Tanner was driving a piece of metal into the bung of a new barrel, then turning the tap to allow more ale to flow into the large jug from which he could fill the pots.

'Leave the talking to me,' Edward insisted, then he called out to Tanner. 'We're looking for Ellie!'

'Well, she isn't here, is she?' Tanner replied without taking his eyes off what he was doing.

'Who's this lady?' Edward asked.

'The missus — her name's Joan. Don't even think about jumping the queue. She doesn't like the authorities any more than I do, and she's not as fast as poor old Ellie.'

'Why "poor old Ellie"?' Edward demanded.

Tanner seemed to be concentrating on the delicate task of refilling the jug rather than thinking his answers through carefully. 'Well, I mean — getting herself murdered like that. She obviously went with the wrong mark.'

'And what makes you think she's been murdered?' Edward demanded.

Tanner looked confused. 'Well, I mean — she must have been. I've never known her to miss work. She was too fond of the pennies, that one. Why else would she have gone missing for three days?'

'I think you know *precisely* why, Master Tanner,' Edward thundered, 'and I intend to exercise my authority to search your premises.'

'Search all you like,' Tanner growled, 'but mind you don't steal anything.'

For the next hour, Edward and Francis made a thorough search of the entire premises, including the back corridor in which they disturbed several patrons with local doxies. But they found nothing, despite making a thorough examination of the cupboard that they pulled out from its position at the end of the passageway. It revealed a securely locked and heavily studded oak door that refused to yield to their attempts to get it open.

Tanner grinned mockingly as they reappeared in the taproom. 'You found nothing, did you?' he taunted.

Edward glared back as he shouted, 'I'll make sure that what goes on in that rear passageway is reported to the magistrates!'

'Please yourself,' Tanner cackled back, 'but some of them are good customers.'

As Edward and Francis stormed out through the back store that gave access to the side alleyway, Edward raised his hand to indicate that they should halt. He then pointed to the floor. 'How does that differ from the rest of this disgusting establishment, would you say?'

'Well, it's clean, for one thing,' Francis replied.

Edward nodded. 'Precisely. Someone's gone to a great deal of trouble to sluice this floor clean. Help me lift these large brewer's barrels.'

They struggled to raise the huge wooden containers an inch or two off the ground, and on the third attempt Edward gave a shout of triumph.

'See here, under the rim! See that brown mark formed by the metal rim? If that isn't dried blood, then I don't know my business. Whoever cleaned this place only did a slipshod job, and that would be typical of a filthy villain like Tanner.'

'If we ask him to explain, he'll no doubt say it came from an animal carcass, or that he cut himself or something,' Francis observed gloomily.

'But at least we know how — and where — that poor young woman met her fate. All we have to do now is prove it.'

'Good luck with that,' Francis replied with a downcast face, 'but I have to admire your determination. So is it back to the Guildhall?'

'No, the castle, I think. Tomorrow I have to put together the posse that will clear the North Road ahead of Cecil's renewed journey, and I'll need to speak with the garrison commander about co-operating with his escort.'

'Leaving me to make further enquiries about the murder of Ellie?'

'Officially, yes. But unofficially it might be a good idea to find out more about what lies inside that castle rock. If my local knowledge — such as it is — serves me right, there were once dungeons down there, which must have passageways leading down from the castle itself. And those weren't the ghosts of long dead children we heard wailing last night. I believe that our missing women may be down there somewhere.'

'Why can't we just ask Waldegrave to make a search?'

'Because we don't know if he himself is behind the disappearances, do we? The best time for you to go looking will be while he's on the North Road with me, ensuring the safety of Robert Cecil. I'll leave that to you.'

'Thank you for nothing at all,' Francis grumbled. 'I hope it pours with rain for the whole of Friday.'

8

Edward turned in the saddle and looked back, to ensure that he and his posse were keeping the correct distance ahead of Colonel Waldegrave and his castle escort, behind whom would be Master Cecil and his entourage. The road they were travelling was taking them on a winding route through the densest part of Sherwood Forest, and there were modern outlaws to beware of, who infested every lonely track in the nation.

After the defeat of the Armada, Queen Elizabeth had lost no time in discharging her navy, condemning to poverty and unemployment the thousands of mariners who had lined the decks of her proud vessels. Many of those men were now minus arms, legs and eyesight, unable to provide for their families by any means other than robbing those who wandered on the highways.

This was why Edward had been commanded to ensure that these surly and murderous bands were not present when Robert Cecil and his party headed for their next overnight destination, Sheffield Manor. The Colonel of Nottingham Castle had provided additional protection to the courtly traveller on his journey north, and Edward had therefore commissioned a dozen men to be part of his posse, all local farmers with sufficient wealth to possess both horses and swords. They were now spread out across the winding road as it snaked through coppices of oak, beech and fir, and they cast wary eyes into the thick bracken that could hide a man intent on springing out on an unsuspecting victim.

Colonel Waldegrave had made several attempts to dissuade Edward from carrying out his orders, which Edward himself put down to the pompous man's desire for glory and recognition of his service to the Crown. Waldegrave, unknown to Edward, had even gone so far as to write to Sheriff Thornhough with the polite suggestion that since he and his garrison were more than a match for desperate beggars lurking in the undergrowth, the county might best deploy its bailiff on more urgent matters. Thornhough, who knew Waldegrave for the ingratiating braggart that he was, had not even deigned to reply, and so the colonel had been required to minimise the loss of face by instructing Edward to keep his posse at least a quarter of a league ahead of the main party. To maximise this distancing, Edward had been ordered out to collect his posse at daybreak on the Friday, and meet up with the main party when it reached Bestwood Lodge. This was convenient for him, since most of his men were drawn from the rural areas north of the town. They had been joined at Bestwood by Waldegrave and an advanced detachment of mounted men at arms from the main party, and ordered northward at least a quarter of a league ahead.

As they spread out and wound their way up the dusty track with the encroaching forest on either side of them, they became aware of groups of starved-looking men who glared at them through the dense foliage, but only one group was bold enough to step out in front of them and demand to know their business. Edward replied in a loud and commanding voice that his business was none of theirs, but nevertheless he informed them that he rode with his men ahead of a larger troop of royal soldiers, escorting the queen's emissary to Scotland. This was enough to send them skulking back to their hiding place with a few muttered curses.

Waldegrave had instructed them to halt when they came to Rufford Abbey, since this was where Cecil's party was expected to pause for a meal in the middle of the day. This was well over halfway to the county border, where the main party would join the Great North Road, then turn westwards for their overnight destination. At this point, Edward's posse would turn back for Nottingham at Bawtry, having seen their courtly charge safely through the county. The sun was therefore well past its height when the main cavalcade clattered into the forecourt of the abbey. Waldegrave rode over to where Edward sat with his men on a grassy bank to advise him that they would be fed and watered in the converted hospitium of the former abbey, now one of the homes of the Earl of Shrewsbury, who would also be hosting Cecil at Sheffield Manor later that day.

As Edward's collection of farmers turned soldiers scuttled happily off in search of their food, he had his first view of the main party that had been behind them for the entire morning. His attention was drawn to three covered litters that appeared to be part of Cecil's travelling retinue. Such conveyances were normally reserved for ladies of noble or royal lineage travelling with their menfolk. Edward had noticed, upon their arrival, that they had been in the centre of the procession, closely guarded, and that their covers were tied down, denying their occupants either fresh air or a view of their surroundings. His curiosity got the better of him, and he wandered across to one of them and unfastened the rope that was holding down the canvas.

To his amazement, he found himself staring down at a solitary occupant lying flat on the board inside the litter, who was clearly not of noble or royal lineage, to judge by her simple yellow gown and the lack of any headdress. However, her hair, dyed deep red, was impossible to miss, and his memory flew back to the girl he had seen cavorting in one of the enclaves at The Crusader. As he stood staring at her, her eyes opened and she blinked in the wintry sunlight.

Reasoning that she had almost certainly entered the litter in Nottingham, Edward asked, 'Who are you?'

'Emma. Emma Partridge,' the woman replied.

'Do you know a young woman called Nell Franklin?' he asked.

She pointed a finger at somewhere in her imagination. 'In that other one.'

'Did Richard put you in here?'

She nodded as her eyes closed again. 'Help us, please.'

'Get away from there!' a voice commanded.

Edward turned to find himself staring into the eyes of Colonel Waldegrave. 'These women have been abducted, haven't they?' Edward demanded. He froze as Waldegrave drew his sword and pointed it threateningly at his chest.

'Come with me,' the colonel instructed, and Edward turned and trudged angrily in the direction indicated, conscious of the blade only inches from his back as he headed towards the building in which everyone was presumably dining.

They reached the front entrance hall, which was being guarded by two of Waldegrave's men in their livery. Edward was reminded again of the red and white patterned cloth he'd found under the table in The Crusader.

'Keep this man under close guard,' Waldegrave commanded them as he strode on towards the great hall from which the noise of merrymaking could be heard. 'If he makes any effort to escape, run him through!'

A few minutes later, Waldegrave reappeared in the company of a man half his height. His furtive face was heavily pockmarked, and his gait reminded Edward of a freshwater shellfish. The man looked Edward up and down with a disdainful glare and asked in a reedy voice, 'Why were you looking inside that litter?'

'Those women have been abducted, have they not?' Edward demanded.

The man's lips twisted in a snarl. 'What women would they be?'

'The ones in the litters out there. They were taken against their will from The Crusader tavern in Nottingham, after being seduced by a man called Richard, who promised them a better life in London. Where are you taking them and why? I speak with the authority of the Sheriff of Nottinghamshire, whose bailiff I am.'

'And have you any idea of whom you are speaking *to*?' his inquisitor asked.

By now, Edward had guessed whom he was dealing with. 'I believe you to be Robert Cecil, son of Sir William Cecil.'

Cecil nodded. 'The son of Baron Burghley, as he is now known, formerly the secretary to Her Majesty Queen Elizabeth, and the foremost of her courtiers. I travel on his business, and the contents of those litters are part of that business.'

'He's taken to managing a brothel?'

'Silence, you impudent scum!' Cecil ordered angrily. 'It is not for you to challenge how the business of this realm is conducted in Her Majesty's name. You are familiar with the penalties for treason or sedition?'

'Death by the axe,' Edward replied as he stared defiantly back at the obnoxious little man, determined to show no fear.

'The axe is for those towards whom Her Majesty is feeling generous,' Cecil said. 'Those who annoy her are first hanged to the point of death, then taken down while still alive and disembowelled.'

'And why do you kindly take the trouble to advise me of that?'

'Because it will be your fate should you breathe a word of what you have witnessed today. Those women are meant as a sweetening device when we engage certain members of the Scottish Court, where it is in Her Majesty's best interests that we be received with an honourable welcome.'

'Even though the so-called "gifts" that you bear be *far* from honourable?' Edward defied him. 'Does Her Majesty condone what you are about? Does she stoop so low in her conduct of affairs of state that she condemns young women to be the slaves of depraved violators?'

Cecil's face grew alarmingly red as he struggled to reply, and Waldegrave attempted to cover his temporary incapacity.

'I will take him out and have him run through, my lord.'

'You will do no such thing, you fool!' Cecil bellowed. 'You forget that he is not simply some inconsequential oaf whose death would go unnoticed. He is an agent of the sheriff through whose county we are travelling, and investigations into his demise in such a violent fashion would lead to inconvenient questions. It is not as if we are engaged in anything that threatens Her Majesty's grip on power, so let him go free.'

'Free to tell the world what he has witnessed?'

'And who would be likely to believe his word against ours? Added to which, should he speak out of turn, thereby slandering one of Her Majesty's most trusted ambassadors, he may be taken to be seeking to undermine Her Majesty's authority. You may take it from me that this is not a matter that she would regard lightly.'

'I will of course defer to your more experienced judgement in these matters,' Waldegrave muttered.

Cecil glared up at Edward. 'You heard what I just said, fool. One word of any of this — to *anyone* — and I will know where any inconvenient rumours originated, and have you taken up on a charge of treason or sedition. Either way, the end result will be the same, and very messy. Now, go back to where you crawled from.'

He turned on his heel and headed back to the banquet, leaving Waldegrave staring at Edward in disbelief.

'Trust me, Master Mountsorrel, when I assure you that you just had a very narrow escape from one of the most dangerous men in the kingdom.'

'Also one of the most dishonourable,' Edward sneered, 'but you cannot expect me to neglect my duty to such an extent as to abandon these poor women to whatever dreadful fate awaits them.'

'They are *prostitutes*, you cretin!' Waldegrave thundered. 'Why should you risk all for the sake of women who sell their bodies for pennies?'

'I make no moral judgements in the execution of my solemn duty,' Edward replied, 'and these unfortunate women are being held against their will, and consigned to a place where they will be constantly violated. At least as prostitutes they could choose their own marks and set their own prices.'

Waldegrave shook his head. 'You will never progress far in public life with scruples of that nature. Nor will you live one more day if you seek to reveal what you have witnessed. Should you do so, I shall think of some good reason why I was obliged to run you through, or have you hanged, and I am in far higher standing with those who matter than you are, so who will disbelieve me? Now, take your men, go back to

Nottingham, and await me there. I shall be watching your every move — and that of your friend Barton.'

Appreciating that there was nothing to be gained from further argument, Edward collected his posse from where they had been filling their stomachs and advised them that the colonel had graciously undertaken to escort the queen's ambassador to the county boundary, and that they were free to return to their homes.

The last of them bid him goodbye just south of Bulwell village, leaving Edward to take the track down to Basford just as sun went down, leaving a full moon to light his way. He tied his horse to the fence outside Sheriff Thornhough's fine house and walked down the front path to the door. A somewhat reluctant steward admitted him as far as the entrance lobby, then left him warming his feet by stamping them on the wooden blocks until a visibly annoyed Thornhough came down the hall.

'I was about to take my supper. Why are you here?' he demanded. 'Has something gone awry during your escort duties for Master Cecil? If so, it will not be to your advantage.'

Edward took a deep breath. 'Master Cecil was escorted as far as Rufford Abbey, then I was ordered by Colonel Waldegrave to turn back, since he had sufficient men to safely continue the journey north. I did not know that he was also commanded to accompany Master Cecil.'

'Neither did I when I gave you your instructions, but is that all you have to report? If so, be gone, and leave me to my supper.'

'There is more, I regret to say,' Edward persisted. 'Master Cecil has, in his retinue, at least five prostitutes from the town who have been abducted by him and taken north.'

'So he has lusty pursuits — what of that?'

'These women did not go willingly, sir. In fact, I believe them to have been overpowered by poison while being seduced by an agent of Cecil's in a low tavern below the castle rock. They were then taken against their will on the journey north.'

'They are prostitutes, say you?' Thornhough asked testily. 'Why should we concern ourselves with town doxies?'

'They did not wish to be abducted, sir. That is a matter of which we must take note, and a matter on which we must act, since these dreadful crimes occurred within the county.'

'And what precisely do you propose? That we summon a posse, ride north, and deprive one of Her Majesty's favourites of a handful of prostitutes?'

Edward nodded with resignation. 'I am simply reporting to you that certain low crimes were committed within your jurisdiction, as I am obliged to do as part of my duties.'

'Committed by whom, do you say?'

'In the first instance by the proprietor of the alehouse in question — a low person called Tanner. I believe that he was complicit in allowing his premises to be used by the seducer, who goes by the name of Richard and is most likely employed by Cecil. I also believe Tanner murdered a young woman who served the ale in his disreputable den, after overhearing her when she alerted me to what was going on. Finally, I suspect Colonel Waldegrave turned a blind eye to these women being conveyed north. He was clearly not surprised when I confronted Cecil with my suspicions.'

'You did *what*?' Thornhough shrieked, but Edward was not to be intimidated.

'I confronted Cecil with my discovery of one of the women, in a drugged state, in one of several closed litters that were travelling north in his cavalcade.'

'And what was his reaction?'

'He threatened to have me hung, drawn and quartered if I told a soul what I had learned.'

'As you have just told me?'

'I do not believe that you will betray me, and I seek your authority to ride back north and have these women released.'

'I will not betray you, principally because it would not go well for me if Cecil were to learn that you have passed on these evil tidings. Ensure that you tell no-one that you have confided in me. But I do not intend to imperil my life and my future fortune for the sake of a handful of fallen women.'

'So you intend to do nothing about what I have learned?'

'No, and neither are you to do anything, do you understand? Your position as my bailiff already hangs by a thread, and if you take one further step in this matter, you will no longer occupy that office. Do I make myself clear?'

'Yes, sir,' Edward all but spat.

Thornhough gave him a wan smile as he turned to go back down the hall. 'I would invite you to share my supper, only I do not wish to be associated with someone who carelessly puts his head so close to the block. Goodnight, Master Mountsorrel.'

While Edward had been learning some hard lessons about the realities of political power, Francis had been investigating as instructed. After a late breakfast, he strolled around the main building to its western terrace, which offered a view across the north of the town and was the entrance point for the castle dungeons. A metal gate had been left open on its hinges, and immediately behind that was a studded oak door.

After looking quickly behind him to check that he was unobserved, Francis pushed on the door, which yielded to his touch, revealing a dank, downward corridor through the rock.

He had no torch, and it was obvious that once he turned the sharp corner to the right a few feet down the corridor, there would be no more natural light. Rather than risk a challenge if he went back into the daylight in search of a torch, Francis continued downwards.

Once the light failed he was in almost total darkness, which became more intense the further he walked along the rutted floor. Swift progress was impossible, and he could only feel his way if he put out his hands and felt along the crumbling sandstone. So far as he could tell, the slope took him predominantly to the right, heading round the inside of the rock towards the east side of the castle. From time to time his outstretched hand came to rest on a solid oak door set in the sandy rock, which he took to be the door to a dungeon. He shuddered as he imagined the mental agony of the poor wretches left inside these pitch-black caverns. From time to time he became aware of a startled scuttling sound as something slipped furtively over his boot, and he had a suspicion that someone was following closely behind him.

With an almost overpowering sense of relief, he felt a gap open up to his left, and as he explored it with his left glove, he found a half open oak door. It must, he reasoned, be the door to one of these prison cells, and if he slipped inside he could perhaps wait while whoever was pursuing him went on down the tunnel. So he stepped inside as silently as he could.

Almost immediately he tripped on something, and a foul stench assailed his nostrils as something slimy spilled over his boot. He'd visited enough prison cells to recognise the stench of bodily waste, and he gagged just as the door that he had gone through slammed shut behind him, and he heard the rasp of a key turning in the lock. He'd been correct in believing that he'd been followed, and now here he was, deep in the castle rock without food or water. There was only one way he could draw attention to his plight, but that would have to wait for Edward's return.

9

Back at the castle, Edward threw his riding gloves down on his bed in disgust and went in search of something to eat, anxious to pass on the dreadful tidings to Francis. The narrow, airless room in which food was normally made available to the castle occupants was gloomy and empty, with only one torch in its bracket on the outer stone wall beside the grimy mullioned window. Edward therefore wandered into the kitchen in the hope that something had been left out by the cook for those who were on late duties.

Munching despondently on a piece of stale black bread, he wondered where Francis might be, and what he might have discovered about the role that had been played by the castle and its colonel in the disappearance of the women. Edward returned to their shared bedchamber, noting with mounting unease that Francis still hadn't arrived back. He then fell onto his straw bedding and was soon deeply asleep after all the exertions of the day.

The following morning, Edward's first thought was for Francis. When he saw the empty bolster alongside his, he rose swiftly and wandered downstairs towards the east terrace.

As he stood gazing out across the Meadows towards the Trent, he was reminded that he and Francis still needed to make further enquiries into the murder of Ellie. As his thoughts drifted towards his initial suspicion that Tanner, or someone employed by him, had overheard Ellie talking to him, he looked down towards the base of the massive rock on which the castle perched. At its foot was The Crusader. He was considering ways in which he might approach the authorities to have it closed down, when he heard heavy footsteps behind him, and turned to find Colonel Waldegrave only a few feet away.

'In view of what occurred yesterday, I want you and your companion Barton out of the castle by sundown,' Waldegrave announced. 'You are no longer welcome here, and I will not be seen to be giving sanctuary to someone who has made such an enemy of Master Cecil.'

'We have nowhere else to go,' Edward reminded him coldly, 'which is the only reason that we tolerate the most uncomfortable lodgings that I personally have ever occupied, even as a soldier on the march from one place to another. If we had somewhere else to go — even a piggery — believe me when I tell you that we would leave here with alacrity. And Bailiff Barton has done nothing to annoy anyone, so far as I am aware.'

'Even so…' Waldegrave began, then stopped suddenly when an eerie cry for help drifted up from somewhere below them.

'What was that?' Edward demanded as the cry was repeated, more desperately this time. When Waldegrave remained silent, Edward stepped forward, grasped the collar of the colonel's tunic, and twisted. 'That was Francis Barton's voice, was it not? Don't try to persuade me that it was another of your so-called ghosts, because I have worked with the man, and shared a house with him, for the best part of a year. You have him locked away somewhere, don't you?'

'You are obviously still fatigued after your long journey yesterday,' Waldegrave attempted to suggest.

'Not so fatigued that I failed to notice that Francis has been missing since I returned. Release him immediately!'

'You may search the dungeons all you wish, but you will not find him,' Waldegrave insisted, 'and if you do not unhand me immediately, I'll run you through! Then my men will take your bleeding remains and throw them off this rock. Unhand me *now!*'

Edward did as requested, but then drew his sword. 'I have not lost my skills with this trusty blade that I have wielded for Her Majesty, and I shall not hesitate to use it on you should you choose to draw yours as you threaten. In fact, it would give me the greatest pleasure to plunge it through your innards, you treacherous dog!'

Waldegrave smiled nastily. 'You forget that this castle is occupied by men under my command, who will not hesitate to fall upon you should you lay a hand on me. Then they will take great pleasure in casting you into the same hole in which your dear friend will no doubt languish until he suffers a slow death. It is hardly my fault if he took it upon himself to spy on my activities in my absence and fell into one of the many traps for the unwary that are to be found within this rock. If you wish to be reunited with him, go ahead and engage me in swordplay!'

'At least you have confirmed where Francis may be found,' said Edward as he backed away and made a run for the stables in which his horse was being kept. He threw on the saddle, tightened the girth, grabbed the reins and launched himself onto the animal's back. He then cantered out into the parade square, scattering armed men in all directions, and thundered under the gatehouse archway before those guarding it had time to bar the gate.

As he pulled the horse back into a gentle clop down Whitefriars Lane, past where their new house sat half constructed while labourers awaited the delivery of the roof timbers, Edward thought quickly. Francis was obviously imprisoned somewhere *inside* the castle rock, probably in the same place that the women had been held. There was clearly a passageway between that dungeon and the castle that had allowed the litters to be loaded with the women before they had been taken north. But if it was assumed that the women had been thrown into their temporary dungeon from *inside* The Crusader, then there had to be a linking tunnel from somewhere within it. The way into that was almost certainly behind the heavy oak door concealed by the cupboard.

To judge by the angle of the sun it was approaching mid-morning, and Edward needed more men if he was to invade The Crusader and force open the suspect door. As the county bailiff he had no direct authority over the town constables, and his own men were few in number and spread throughout the rural villages. But Francis was popular with his men, and Edward had little doubt that they would come to his assistance. He quickened his horse's pace and nudged him through the already bustling marketplace before heading south down Bridlesmith Gate and into Low Pavement, where the Guildhall was located.

The sight of the market traders setting up their stalls, and a handful of local residents moving through them in search of early bargains, reminded him that it was Saturday — market day. The town constables would be gathering inside the Guildhall ahead of their market patrols in search of pickpockets, prostitutes and cut-purses. He might just be in time if he delayed no longer. He threw the horse's looped bridle over a gatepost and raced inside the main building from which Nottingham was administered.

He was in luck, and five minutes later he was leading a party of five down Low Pavement and into Greyfriars, at the end of which the dusty track gave way to boggy meadow, which they crossed in order to enter the Rockyard from the east. The Crusader was not yet open for business, which would make things easier for them, and it was with a sense of mounting elation that Edward hammered on the side door of the premises with his sword hilt, and turned to order the men behind him to storm in as soon as the door opened.

A bleary-eyed Jebediah Tanner stared in amazement as his rear storage vault filled with constables armed with their staffs of office. Edward stuck a sword tip under his nose for long enough to advise him that he was under arrest on suspicion of murder. A demand for his keys was met with a sullen sneer, so Edward instructed that a thorough search be conducted throughout the premises, and that every key found be brought to him. When satisfied that they probably had them all, Edward ordered two of his accompanying constables to ensure that Tanner didn't escape, then took the remainder with him as he ran into the side passageway with three bundles of keys in his hands.

He ordered the men to heave aside the cupboard, thereby exposing the heavy oak door. He looked carefully at the keyhole, then tried each of the keys that still appeared to be shiny through constant use until he was able to turn one in the heavy lock. With a shout of joy, he heaved the door open with his shoulder.

'Bring me some light!' he called out. One of the men ran back out to the front door, where a torch had been burning down from the night before. Edward took it from him and began the slow and frustrating upward climb through the sandstone corridor that had been revealed once the door had been opened. At regular intervals there were brackets containing torch bundles, and Edward lit them one by one as he worked his way up the slope, calling out for a response from Francis.

Twenty yards up the sandy slope was another heavy oak door, and from behind it Edward heard Francis's calls in reply to his. After another fumble, he realised that the same key that had opened the door from The Crusader also worked on this dungeon door. Edward walked in, raising his torch to the welcome sight of a dust-coated Francis, who rose to throw his arms around him.

'I think this is where they kept the women,' he whispered hoarsely.

'I *know* it is,' Edward confirmed, 'and you will not be surprised to learn that we shall be leaving by way of The Crusader.' As they made their way back out into the daylight through the side entrance to the tavern, he went on, 'I ordered the arrest of our host here for the murder of Ellie. I fear that I overstepped my authority in that regard, and you may now wish to ensure that matters are conducted properly.'

Francis cheerfully ordered his constables to take Tanner into custody, and they walked up through the Rockyard. 'I never thought that the air in this stinking thoroughfare would smell so sweet,' said Francis. 'Some bastard followed me down from the castle dungeon entrance and locked the door on me. Did you hear my calls?'

'Two of them,' said Edward. 'You made a very unconvincing ghost. But I must advise you that we are homeless. I have much to tell you of my experiences while you were locked up, but you should know immediately that the missing women are being carried north in the train of Robert Cecil as he travels to Scotland. The poor wretches are meant as gifts for its king.'

'And why does that make us homeless?' Francis asked.

Edward's face fell. 'I confronted Cecil with my discovery, and he threatened to have me conveyed to the Tower for a grisly death if I breathed a word. Then Colonel Waldegrave — who was the one who caught me investigating the litters in which the women were being conveyed — ordered me back south. He was clearly a party to the entire business, and when he returned to the castle he advised me that we are no longer welcome there.'

By this time they had reached the Guildhall, and Edward made to untie his horse before Francis called out to him.

'I don't know about you, but I'm very hungry and thirsty. We can send one of the men out to the pie stand back there, and we have some small beer in the back room. It's so cold at this time of year that it feels like drinking ice.'

Half an hour later, Edward was smiling contentedly and assuring Francis that his accommodation was much better than the equivalent provided for the county officers up the road in the Shire Hall.

'It's perhaps as well,' Francis replied, 'since unless you have any better ideas, it looks as if we'll be bedding down here for a night or two. I have in mind the duty room, in which the constables gather before being allocated their duties. There's always a fire kept burning in there, and the floor is wooden, so it retains some of the heat.'

'I don't think we have much choice,' said Edward, 'but we both need to retrieve what few belongings we have left from the castle. Given the circumstances in which I recently departed from there, I don't think I'd be afforded a very warm welcome.'

'I'd be delighted to retrieve yours along with mine,' Francis offered. 'I want to see Waldegrave's face when I ride in there with two constables in attendance and demand the return of our property. If you're right about his involvement in the abduction of the women, he'll be expecting me to die in that dungeon, and he may take me for a ghost when I ride back in with a smile.'

'He might not let you out again,' Edward warned him.

Francis shook his head. 'Of course he will, since he won't want to antagonise me further, in case I demand that his entire cave network be closed down.'

'Only I have the authority to demand that,' Edward reminded him.

'Agreed. But does *he* know that?'

Francis was back before the middle of the day, carrying both his possessions and Edward's in a large travelling bag that had been donated by Waldegrave himself.

'He gave it to me to make up for the "unfortunate accident" that befell me when one of his men mistook me for an intruder,' Francis chuckled. 'Complete nonsense, of course. What do you intend to do about the abducted women, Edward?'

Edward shrugged. 'How do you suggest I stand up against one of the most powerful men at court?'

'I know little of this Robert Cecil,' Francis admitted, 'although I have obviously heard of his more famous father. What did you make of him?'

'He was a repulsive little man, with a face like a pitted pear. He stands no higher than my chest, and he struts around as if he were the queen herself.'

'This must surely make him unpopular in certain quarters?' Francis suggested. 'From the little I have heard of life at court, it is a hotbed of intrigue, back-stabbing and scrabbling for favour.'

'I do not even know that much,' said Edward, then suddenly his eyes opened wide. 'Unless … that is … perhaps…'

'What have you remembered?' Francis prompted him.

'The lady with whom I walked in the gardens at Wollaton Hall — Elizabeth Porter — is privy to all the private family conversations by virtue of her position as lady's maid to the daughter of Sir Francis. She told me of the rivalry between Cecil and the Earl of Essex, who is the stepson of my former benefactor the Earl of Leicester.'

'For someone who claims to know little of courtly life, you seem to be well informed,' said Francis, 'but what use may you make of this knowledge?'

'Elizabeth informs me that Essex is due to visit Wollaton on Tuesday. If I can somehow convey to him the wickedness that Cecil is engaged in, he may seek to use it to his advantage, and secure the rescue of the women.'

'Assuming that you are correct,' Francis frowned, 'I can see two difficulties. The first is that you are not welcome on the Wollaton estate, and the second is that by the time you prod Essex into action — always assuming that you can — the women will be well over the border into Scotland, and lost to us.'

'As to the former, I have twice already managed to meet with Elizabeth in secret without being detected by Sir Francis, so I will hazard it again. As for the second, I must clearly lose no time in speaking with Essex. Cecil bided for several days in Nottingham, so who knows where else he may choose to dally on his way north?'

'I can only wish you luck,' Francis said doubtfully, 'but today is only Saturday. You must wait at least two more days before Essex even arrives at Wollaton, assuming that he is not delayed by other business. And do not forget that on Monday we must attend the funeral of poor old Dickon. I managed to alert his sister here in town, but I have had no response from Kinoulton, so we must be there to ensure that he is not forgotten as he is lowered into the ground.'

'That leaves me tomorrow, does it not?' Edward smiled. 'I think I might take myself off then for another meeting with Mistress Porter. Believe me when I say that this will be no hardship.'

10

Amy looked up from where she was rolling pastry when she heard the kitchen door opening. She smiled when she recognised Edward and wiped her hands down her apron. Looking slyly across at the cook, who was busy plucking a game bird with her back turned, Amy sidled over to the door, pushing Edward gently outside.

'We're both taking a risk,' she whispered, 'but I'll pretend I came out for more flour from the store. What do you want?'

'An urgent meeting with Elizabeth,' Edward whispered. 'Tell her that I shall be in the coppice of trees to the left of the herd-master's hut. Please urge upon her that it is a matter of the utmost importance.'

He slipped back down the path from the kitchen door, bending low behind a yew hedge so as not to be visible from the house as he made his way down the slope. He then ran for the cover of the coppice to wait, and then turned in surprise and alarm when he heard the rustle of branches being pushed aside. Elizabeth sidled further into the clump of oaks in which Edward had concealed himself, kissed him lightly on the cheek, then stepped back and smiled.

'Are you so enamoured of me that you could not wait for another meeting? You were fortunate that my lady is at church with the rest of the family, and that I was excused on account of this fever that causes my nose to drip.'

'I was indeed eagerly anticipating our next meeting,' Edward told her, 'but circumstances have obliged me to bring this about more speedily.'

'And what are they, pray?'

'Is the Earl of Essex still anticipated on Tuesday, two days hence?'

'He is indeed, as I already advised you. But why did you need confirmation of that?'

'I must meet with him as a matter of urgency. It concerns the welfare — and perhaps the lives — of five women from the town.'

'And what is your business with five town women?' Elizabeth asked, slightly put out.

'They have been kidnapped by Robert Cecil and taken north as part of his entourage. They are being taken to the King of Scotland as gifts.' Edward hesitated. 'Forgive the unpleasantness, but they are being taken against their will. I believe that they have been drugged and abducted, to become slaves to the lusts of Scottish courtiers.'

Elizabeth's hand flew to her mouth, and her face reddened. 'That is awful! Unthinkable! Such wickedness — but what is that to do with us?'

'With you, nothing other than assisting me to a meeting with the Earl of Essex, whom I hope might be persuaded to prevent it happening. He is, as you told me during our last meeting, a rival of Robert Cecil?'

'So it is said, but I speak only from what I have heard around the board while attending my lady. I have no knowledge of my own as to how matters proceed at court.'

'Be that as it may, I must attempt to persuade him to ride north and intercept Cecil before he reaches the Scottish border. But in order to do that, I must speak with him.'

'But you are banished from the estate, are you not?'

'Indeed I am, but I do not think that your master will set the dogs on me while I am engaged in conversation with his honoured guest.'

'But how may you achieve that without the master knowing?'

'At this moment, I have no idea,' Edward admitted, 'but I must try.'

'You would risk being ripped apart by the master's fierce hounds for the sake of a handful of local women?' Elizabeth pouted. 'You must be exceeding fond of them.'

'In truth, I have only set eyes on one of them,' Edward told her. 'You forget my calling as county bailiff, sworn to uphold the law.'

'But these are town women, are they not?'

'They are, but their abduction took place in a low tavern that falls within the county. I am duty-bound to prevent Cecil carrying out his wicked scheme.'

'Clearly you take your duties seriously,' said Elizabeth, frowning. 'How do you think I may be able to assist you in gaining an audience with the Earl of Essex?'

'I need to know when I might come upon the earl while he is abroad, rather than cooped up in the hall itself.'

Elizabeth's brow furrowed momentarily, then her eyes lit up. 'I may be able to assist you in that already! The master is proud of his large estate, and seeks to use the earl as a means of persuading Her Majesty to visit here. She is known for her love of horse-riding and hunting. The master plans to take the earl on a tour of the entire grounds, including the deer park and the lake, after dinner on his first day. The earl is staying in Derby on his journey here, and he will be with us by the middle of the morning on Tuesday. I know this because I have been tasked with ensuring that my lady's riding apparel is suitably clean for the occasion.'

'Excellent!' Edward murmured. 'I am greatly in your debt, mistress.'

'Sufficiently in my debt to call me by my first name?'

'Indeed, thank you most profoundly, Elizabeth.'

'And does your debt extend to giving me a kiss?'

'It does indeed, and I shall take pleasure in doing that, if you will present your cheek.'

'My cheek still burns with the embarrassment of learning of the likely fate of the abducted women, so it will have to be my lips.'

Edward took a deep breath, stepped forward, and kissed a woman on the lips for the first time. As he walked away, he was asking himself why he had waited so long to do so.

John Simpson, Rector of St Nicholas's Church across from the castle, threw the first handful of soil onto the winding sheet in which Richard Keyworth — or Dickon, as he was more commonly known — was wrapped for his burial. He then stepped back to allow the four mourners to do likewise as he intoned the final blessing. Young Dickon had only been in his mid-twenties, and the two bailiffs he had so loyally served had been joined by his only surviving relative, his sister Emma, and her husband. The grey cloud that loomed over them was threatening the first snowfall of the year, and the sexton and his boy were waiting to complete the filling in of the grave before the first flakes began to descend.

The man who had been Dickon's brother-in-law walked slowly over to where Edward and Francis stood with bowed heads and held out his hand in a gesture of friendship. 'I must thank you gentlemen most heartily for your kindness to poor Dickon. He spoke highly of your concern for his welfare, and he was proud to be of service to you both.'

'He was highly valued and respected,' Francis replied, wiping a tear from his eye. 'I only wish that there could have been more here today to honour his passing.'

'There was only my wife,' the man replied, 'and I have not yet introduced myself properly. My name is Ralph Tolney. As you must know, having gone to the trouble of advising me of Dickon's death and today's burial, I conduct a fulling enterprise here in Wheelwright Lane, barely yards from where we stand. My wife Emma was Dickon's older sister, and he would visit us on his days off from your service. He was a most likeable lad, and I thought of him as my brother also, despite the difference in our years.'

'There are no other family members?' Francis asked.

Ralph shook his head. 'His parents died of the sweating sickness when it came through their village some years ago. There are, I believe, cousins in Northampton or some such place, but the farm on which Dickon and Emma were raised was sold for a pittance by the lord of the manor when the rent was due and no-one had any reason to keep up the payments.'

'I am an orphan,' Edward volunteered, 'so I have never known what it is to lose a loved one. However, if the grief I felt at Dickon's passing was anything to judge by, then I must be grateful for that blessing.'

'We are still beyond outrage at the manner of his death,' Francis added. 'The fire was clearly intended for us, and Dickon was, we believe, bravely trying to defend us when he met his end.'

'Is your new house completed?' Ralph asked.

Francis shook his head. 'It still wants a roof. To judge by the weather, this will not be achieved until next spring. In the meantime we are lodging in the Guildhall, should you wish to contact us.'

'You have suitable lodgings there?'

Edward allowed himself a hollow laugh. 'Better, at any rate, than we could enjoy in the Shire Hall, which is where I am based for my work. But as a soldier, I became accustomed to sleeping in hedgerows, so a wooden floor by the fire is a distinct improvement.'

'You sleep on a floor inside the Guildhall?' Ralph repeated, aghast, and when both men sheepishly nodded, he broke into a smile. 'You must permit me to return your many kindnesses to poor Dickon. I have a spacious dwelling that comes with the business I inherited from my father, where I was raised. There are two spare chambers on the uppermost floor, and Emma is a good hostess. I would be honoured if you would agree to take up residence with us until your new house is completed.'

Edward and Francis exchanged relieved looks, and a few moments later they accompanied Ralph from the church to his finely appointed house, where fires had been burning all day. The maid of all work whom they employed — Martha Gooding — had baked fresh bread to go with the turnip broth that was her speciality.

'This is exceedingly generous of you,' Francis remarked as he tore another chunk off the bread and dipped it into the broth. 'It makes our working lives much more difficult when we have no comfortable home base.'

Ralph looked enquiringly across the table. 'Perhaps you might be of some service to me — if you regard the location of stolen property as part of your duties.'

'I'm sure that these fine gentlemen have more urgent calls upon their time,' Emma murmured, but Francis was feeling generous.

'If the property to which you allude has been stolen, then indeed it becomes part of our business. More appropriately mine, I believe, if the theft was from you, here in the town.'

'Indeed it was,' Ralph confirmed, 'and I can identify the person responsible, although in order to secure him you might have to proceed with stealth.'

'Please enlighten us,' Edward requested. 'If you believe that this thief may be found outside the town boundaries, I would be more than happy to pursue him along with Francis.'

'No,' Ralph told him, 'he resides here in the town, although in that low part of it known as Narrow Marsh.'

Francis groaned. 'If I had a coin for every low ruffian I've been obliged to take in charge from that area of town, I could retire to my own estate.' He glanced sideways at Edward. 'When you rode over Turncalf Bridge in order to view the body of that unfortunate young woman from The Crusader, you perhaps didn't think to look down at the houses beneath. But had you looked, you would have seen perilous timbers, rotting daub and sagging roofs that pass for dwellings. Pestilence and violence thrive there.'

'You fear to go there?' Ralph asked resignedly. 'In truth, I would not think less of you.'

'We fear to go nowhere!' Edward assured him. 'The point that Francis seeks to emphasise is that in such a place it may be more tedious than normal to effect an apprehension, because the criminals will come together to resist the arrest of one of their own. It is often a bloody contest.'

'And one to which I could not ask you to commit yourselves,' Ralph replied sadly. 'Particularly given your courtesy and kindness to Emma and myself.'

'It is rather we who are indebted to you for your hospitality,' Francis insisted, 'so pray tell us more.'

'Well,' Ralph began hesitantly, 'I employed a man called Jack Putnam, a low type, but one with considerable strength and stamina. As you may be aware, the fulling process involves the pounding of raw woollen cloth with hammers or clubs, which requires great physical strength and energy. Jack was one of those who seemed to possess such attributes in abundance, and he was of particular value to me as age began to take its toll. Most fullers like myself are finished by the age of thirty, but I still thrive in a reduced fashion four years after that milestone in my life. We harden the product by soaking it in a mixture of urine and a special earth that may be obtained from a local apothecary; it then has to be dried by further beating, until the final cloth is fit to sell to the dyer.'

'This man Jack Putnam is the one you suspect of stealing from you?' asked Francis.

'Indeed it is, and I have proof,' said Ralph. 'What I need is the service of men such as yourselves who are prepared to risk cracked skulls in order to have him taken in charge.'

'What was the nature of this theft, and what is your proof?' Francis persisted.

'I had begun to notice the disappearance of certain items used in my trade. First it was my best hammer, then a knife used for cutting the ties around bales of raw cloth. Finally, a barrow in which we would transport the product from one process hut to another. I challenged Jack, but he denied any knowledge of the disappearances. Then I learned that on his free days he was making himself available for small carrying tasks around the lower town — bales of finished knitwear, small items of furniture and the like. So I set a trap by adopting an assumed name, borrowing a business address from a friend of mine in Stoney Street, and sending word that I required Jack's services for the carting of leather goods to the Saturday market. When he turned up, he was of course proposing to use my barrow, and I challenged him. He ran off, and I have heard nothing of him since. To add insult to injury, the barrow, when I retrieved it, was heavily stained with blood. He had obviously used it on a prior occasion to transport animal carcasses, or so I assume.'

'Do you have the precise location within Narrow Marsh where we might corner him?' Francis asked.

Ralph shook his head. 'The dwellings down there seem to blend into one stinking mess, but perhaps you might plan to take him when he is out and about in the town.'

'The problem with that is that once we make enquiry of his whereabouts, he will be made aware of our interest in him, and will either go to ground or leave the town,' Francis explained.

Ralph nodded. 'Believe me, I fully perceive the difficulty you face, but should you come across him...'

'Be assured that we will lose no time in tying his arms behind his back,' Francis assured him. 'And now, if you would be so good as to show us to our chambers?'

Ralph led the way up the narrow wooden staircase to the two garret rooms under the eaves. The ceilings sloped down above the mullioned windows that looked out over the street, and each room had the additional few feet of jettied floor that overhung the floor below. Ralph smiled at Francis's obvious delight as he looked round the chamber, then opened the travelling bag he had acquired at the castle.

Edward began taking those items that were his, and was about to walk to the adjoining chamber when he heard a startled shout from Ralph, who was gazing at the sturdy knife that Francis had tipped out onto the bed.

'That knife!' Ralph yelled. 'Where did you get it?'

'Do you recognise it?' Francis asked in a shaking voice.

'Indeed I do!' said Ralph. 'It's mine, although I have not seen it for some weeks. It was among the items stolen from me by Jack Putnam. How, pray, did you come by it?'

Francis dropped his gaze to the floor. 'We found it on the night that our house was set ablaze. I think we now have a good reason of our own to go in search of Jack Putnam. When we found the knife, it was buried deep in Dickon's ribs.'

11

Edward and Francis sat across the table from Ralph in the downstairs room, gloomily considering the implications of what they had just learned. Emma kept up the flow of small beer from the large earthenware jug, sniffling quietly to herself all the while.

'It doesn't seem right,' she eventually said. 'Our own knife, used to kill my brother! It must have been Jack who did it.'

'Not necessarily,' Edward cautioned. 'In my experience, useful items like knives are frequently stolen — as yours was from you — or perhaps loaned out to those who have an evil use for it.'

'Even so,' Ralph observed grimly, 'Jack Putnam must have taken it from us, and it's his fault that it was used to kill poor Dickon.'

'You have a valid point there,' Francis agreed, 'and when I find Master Putnam, he will have several questions to answer. It may even be that your barrow was used in order to carry a body from one place to another. After all, you said that it was heavily stained with blood when you got it back.'

'That could have been animal blood,' Ralph pointed out.

Edward suddenly had another thought. 'How about deer? Dickon was killed, and our house was set on fire, after I made enquiries of that rogue Brackenridge regarding the missing deer from the Wollaton estate. Perhaps Putnam was working for Brackenridge, and used the barrow to cart deer carcasses around. If the deer were fleshly slaughtered once they reached Brackenridge's premises, then there would have been plenty of blood on them. We know that the deer were driven off the

Wollaton estate while still alive, and where could it be more convenient to slit their throats than in Brackenridge's yard — perhaps using your knife, Ralph?'

'We're in danger of making too many assumptions here,' Francis cautioned them. 'For one thing, a man in Brackenridge's trade would have enough knives of his own, without the need to borrow one from someone else.'

'That said, the knife stolen by Putnam was very sharp,' said Ralph. 'I'm very particular regarding the condition in which I keep my tools. And it seems to me that Edward had a valid point about the timing of Dickon's death. You say that you were questioning Brackenridge earlier on the day that your house was set alight?'

'Yes,' Edward confirmed, 'and he was mightily annoyed that I might be about to reveal that he'd supplied stolen venison to Thurland Hall. But was that sufficient reason to have Dickon killed, in an attempt to burn us to death?'

Ralph gave a bitter laugh. 'I wouldn't put anything past Henry Brackenridge in his ambition to become our next mayor. He's already an alderman, and mayors are chosen from their ranks, so it's really just a matter of ensuring that he has more support for his bid than anyone else. This requires him to keep well in with the burgesses like myself, and he's not above a bit of bribery when he sees the opportunity. It's also rumoured that he poisoned the stock-in-trade of one of his chief rivals, the vintner Giles Pockling who used to have that business in Bridlesmith Gate. Two people died as the result of drinking the adulterated wine, and poor old Giles was ruined. So I could well imagine Brackenridge wishing to suppress any suggestion that he was involved with poachers.'

'From what we could see, on the morning after the fire, an attempt had been made to make use of the prevailing wind by setting fire to the kitchen, so it looked like the fire had spread from there accidentally,' said Francis. 'He wasn't to know that Dickon slept in that kitchen.'

'Don't go making excuses for the murdering bastard!' Ralph responded angrily.

'Believe me, I'm not,' Francis assured him. 'I'm merely suggesting that Brackenridge hired someone — perhaps Jack Putnam — to set fire to our kitchen, and that when he set about it, he was challenged by Dickon and was obliged to kill him in order to complete his wicked task.'

Emma gave a strangled cry, put down her serving jug and ran towards the scullery with her hand over her mouth. Francis watched her leave, then apologised to Ralph.

'No need,' Ralph replied, 'since we need to talk these things through if we are to bring Dickon's killer to justice. It seems to me that your next enquiries, gentlemen, must be with Master Brackenridge.'

'Not me,' Edward replied. 'For one thing I have urgent business at Wollaton Hall on the morrow, and for another I have already had dealings with Brackenridge, and he proved most uncooperative.'

'That was in connection with stolen venison,' said Francis. 'He may be far more anxious to clear his name of murder. If I'm correct, and he ordered only the firing of our house and kitchen, then he must have been horrified when he learned that a man other than us had died in the process.'

'So you intend to challenge him with that?' Edward asked sceptically. 'Good luck, is all I can say. Somehow, my self-appointed task of persuading the Earl of Essex to rescue five Nottingham prostitutes from Master Cecil seems less onerous than it did, compared with what you are contemplating.'

As Edward turned his horse into the open Derby Road gate entrance to Wollaton Park, a man stepped out in front of him, armed with a sword.

'State your business,' he demanded.

Edward smiled down at him. 'You are better armed than the last time we met. You are Master Grantham, are you not?'

'That's me, so what are you referring to?'

'The night that you were set upon by those who were driving deer off the estate, I was one of those who came to your rescue. I'm Edward Mountsorrel, bailiff to the Sheriff of Nottinghamshire.'

'Did you catch the poachers yet?'

'Not yet, but that's my business here today. I have to complete my investigations, down by the lake.'

'We've got important visitors up at the hall today.'

'I'm aware of that — the Earl of Essex. Has he arrived yet?'

'Some hours since,' Grantham told him as he stepped to one side. 'On you go, then.'

Edward thanked him and rode slowly down through the deer park until he reached the lake. He then trotted his horse down the path, with the water to his left and a line of beech trees to his right. A few hundred yards down the path, he dismounted and led his horse into the trees, where he tied him to a trunk well out of sight and prepared for the moment he'd been planning.

It was, by his calculation, well over an hour later that he stepped out of his hiding place and peered up the path for the fifth time, to be rewarded by the sight of a group on horseback wending its way down the grassy slope from the Hall. He slid back among the trees and waited for what seemed like an eternity before the group came two abreast over the narrow wooden bridge across the stream that fed into the lake, and he could make out their faces.

First came two mounted soldiers wearing complex livery that Edward took to be that of the Essex family. Immediately behind them rode Sir Francis Willoughby and a handsome bearded man whom Edward took to be Essex himself, dressed as if for the hunt, with a fine brown fustian tunic and matching hose, a darker brown cloak and a green bonnet. The group of women a few yards behind were made up of Elizabeth Porter, an older woman who might well have been Lady Willoughby, and a younger one who was presumably her married daughter. At the rear of the group were several estate workers on foot, who were obliged to trot at a stiff pace in order to keep up with those on horseback.

Sir Francis was waving an arm across the lake when Edward stepped boldly out into the centre of the path, causing the entire party to hurriedly pull on their mounts' reins. The two armed men kicked their horses forward to surround Edward with their swords drawn, while Sir Francis called out in a loud voice.

'Please excuse this unplanned intrusion, my lord. This oaf serves a local law officer, and has been banned from my estate after his failure to prevent the poaching of several deer. If your men would care to secure him, I will have him thrown into the basement of the hall until his employer can see to the matter of his arrest.'

There was a look of amusement on Essex's face, and Edward fancied that he might have welcomed the diversion from Sir Francis's endless prattling about the suitability of the estate for a royal visit. He therefore opted to fill the silence.

'My Lord of Essex?'

'I am he,' said the earl. 'What of it?'

'I am here to warn you of certain behaviour on the part of Robert Cecil that might reflect badly upon him, and might also have implications for Her Majesty's relations with the Scottish king.'

'The man is clearly deranged!' Sir Francis insisted. 'Allow me to have him taken in charge, then we may continue our tour of the estate.'

Essex gave him a cold sideways look as he replied, 'I shall rule on his lunacy once I have heard what he has to say, Willoughby. It might prove to be more of a diversion than your complete inventory of every species of wildlife on your estate that Her Majesty might wish to slaughter.' He smiled encouragingly down at Edward, and enquired as to his office and business.

'I am Edward Mountsorrel, bailiff to the Sheriff of Nottinghamshire, and I am investigating the disappearance of several young ladies from the town.'

'And what has that to do with Robert Cecil?' Essex asked.

Edward took pleasure in nodding towards Sir Francis. 'It might be better if that were disclosed to your ears only, my lord.'

Essex turned to Sir Francis. 'I shall dismount and hear what this man has to say. He may, as you suggest, be bereft of his wits, but the nature of the business he declares is such that I cannot be seen to dismiss it without at least hearing him out.'

Sir Francis glowered while Essex dismounted, signalled for his two armed escorts to accompany him, then waved Edward on with one gloved hand. 'Let us move on a pace, in order that we be not overheard.'

Twenty yards further down the path Essex called a halt, then moved close to Edward and kept his voice low as he asked, 'What have you to reveal regarding the doings of Robert Cecil?'

'My lord,' Edward all but stammered, scarcely able to believe how easy this was turning out to be, 'Robert Cecil was in Nottingham until a few days ago, staying at Thurston Hall for several days as the guest of Sir John Holles.'

'Of this I am aware,' Essex replied testily. 'Pray what has he done against the queen's interests?'

'He has kidnapped five of the town's prostitutes and taken them north, where they are to be presented as gifts to the Scottish king.'

Essex burst out laughing. 'It is rumoured that James of Scotland would be more impressed with a gift of young men.'

'I know nought of that, my lord — simply that these women were taken against their will and will become prisoners should they reach their intended destination. Such behaviour on the part of *anyone* — and I can make no exception, even for someone as exalted as Robert Cecil — is a serious crime, and given that I am both empowered and charged...'

'Yes, yes.' Essex cut him off with an imperious wave of his hand. 'But how reliable is this information of yours?'

'I have seen the women for myself, my lord. They are being conveyed in litters, insensible to their surroundings. I also had it from Master Cecil's own lips — when he had me ejected from the grounds of Rufford Abbey, where he was taking his dinner — that these women were meant as a present for the Scottish king, from Her Majesty Queen Elizabeth.'

'He said that?' Essex asked. 'Those were his precise words?'

'As best as I can recall them,' Edward replied. 'He had me at something of a disadvantage at the time, with a sword at my throat.'

'But he let you live?'

'He suffered me to return south, certainly,' Edward confirmed, 'although he indicated that my life would be forfeit should I recount what I had seen to anyone — yourself included, I must assume.'

'Myself particularly,' Essex grinned. 'You are aware that he and I disagree over certain matters on which we both advise Her Majesty?'

'I have no knowledge of matters at court,' Edward replied diplomatically. 'Nor am I aware of whether or not it is customary for monarchs to exchange prostitutes as a matter of courtesy, but in my understanding of the law, it is a serious crime to take anyone — man or woman — away by force.'

'These women are prostitutes, say you?' Essex asked with evident amusement.

Edward nodded. 'So I am informed. They were seduced, however, by promises of a fine life in London from a man whom I suspect was in the employ of Robert Cecil. It is also my belief that they were drugged by this same man, then held in a dungeon under Nottingham Castle prior to being thrown into those litters and taken north.'

'And when was all this?'

'It was Friday when I laid eyes on the litters and learned what they contained. This was at a place called Rufford Abbey, a good day's ride north of here, and at that time Master Cecil was intending to stay overnight at Sheffield Manor. It is my fear that they may now be to too far ahead of us to be rescued.'

Essex smiled. 'Were you better acquainted with Robert Cecil, you would know that his bodily comfort is his first concern. It would be mine also, were I cursed with a body as crooked as his. He spent several days in Nottingham, you said?'

'Indeed. I was surprised by the length of his stay, if he was indeed on the queen's business, as he claimed to be.'

'He had no business of Her Majesty's of which I am aware,' Essex replied with a sneer, 'since Elizabeth would not entrust him with so much as the supervision of her stables. However, the son does the bidding of the father, and it may be that Baron Burghley was unwise enough to entrust some minor mission to his idiot son. But, being Robert, his bodily comfort will take priority. I have little doubt that he will spend more than one night at each establishment that he favours with his presence. That being so, he may be overtaken in York, where he is known to favour the King's Manor.'

'You will undertake to pursue him and rescue the women?'

'Provided that you accompany me,' Essex replied. 'For one thing you know these women, and for another I need some vestige of authority for intervening.'

'Surely your authority is greater than mine?'

'At court, and in matters of state, it clearly is. But you are a bailiff, and you are investigating a serious breach of the law within your jurisdiction. I suggest that we begin before sunrise tomorrow, if we are to have a reasonable chance of overtaking Cecil and unmasking his devious actions. Can you return here tomorrow, or would it be better for you to stay here overnight?'

'I will need to repair to my lodgings in town for a change of garments, and alert a colleague to what I am about, but I could be back here by sunset.'

'Excellent. Now, let us advise this tedious old fool Willoughby that he can only bore his courtly guest to distraction for one night.'

They walked back along the track to rejoin the perplexed-looking party.

'I must, with regret, cut short my stay with you in order to attend to important matters of state that this gallant young man has brought to my attention,' Essex told Sir Francis. 'We shall need to depart before sunrise tomorrow, and I assume that my companion here may be accommodated somewhere appropriate within the hall once he has returned with certain items that he requires from the town?'

Sir Francis's face glowed with suppressed rage. 'It shall of course be as you wish,' he said through clenched teeth.

In order to keep a straight face, Edward looked towards Elizabeth, who was gazing at him with a broad smile. Then he took his leave as politely as he could and spurred his horse back up the slope.

Francis thought long and hard about how he might set about locating Jack Putnam, and he couldn't escape the reluctant conclusion that he had to begin back at The Dog and Partridge. Interviewing the prostitutes there had always yielded positive results.

'What do you want this time?' Lily Carter demanded when Francis walked into the tavern. 'Couldn't you find some fancy man to take you to London?'

'And have you found Nell Franklin yet?' Tilley Chandler asked as the others giggled.

Francis shook his head. 'That's being looked into by my colleague from the county, Edward Mountsorrel. But you can assist me, if you would, by confirming that there are now five of your friends missing. Nell, obviously, and the last time I was here someone mentioned a girl called Annie Freebourne.'

'That was me,' Jenny Salter reminded him, 'and we haven't seen *her* in here lately, either.'

'Well, I now have three more names for you,' Francis told them as he lifted the crumpled piece of paper from his tunic pocket and read them out loud. 'Jane Ballander, Emma Partridge, and a woman called Mary, whose second name I don't know.'

'I know Jane,' Jenny piped up. 'She normally works round the castle, and sometimes The Crusader, like Nell used to. But not the others, I'm afraid.'

'Same with Emma Partridge, in the old days,' Lily added. 'Then she seemed to get a bit above herself and only worked the big houses in town, like Nell. Just goes to show that it doesn't pay to get above yourself.'

'And none of those women I just named have been in here lately?' Francis asked, and there were shakes of the head all round, so he moved on. 'There's something else I need from you ladies. Do any of you know a man called Jack Putnam?'

'*That* smelly bastard?' Lily responded. 'The one who occasionally does the throwing out in The Crusader? I only have anything to do with him when he's got enough money to make it worth my while to hold my nose for ten minutes, why?'

'Jack Putnam from Narrow Marsh?' Francis persevered.

Lily nodded. 'That's him, but I haven't smelt him in a while. You're looking for him, are you?'

'That's right,' Francis confirmed. 'He's suspected of having stolen some goods from a friend of mine, so he's likely to be spending freely at the moment. If you see him, send word to me at Ralph Tolney's fulling house down on Wheelright Lane.'

'I heard as how your own place got burned down, and with your servant still inside it,' Tilley chimed in. 'Is that why you're lodging with Ralph Tolney?'

'That's right, and keep it to yourselves, but I'm after Jack Putnam for that as well. There'll be a small reward for anyone who can tell me where to find him.'

'You might try that butcher's up on Timber Hill,' Lily said with an outstretched hand. 'I saw him driving one of his wagons a few days back, while I was coming out of the marketplace. How much were you thinking of offering for that reward?'

Francis reached into his pocket and extracted a half groat, which he tossed in Lily's direction.

A short while later, Francis was standing with the butcher in the side yard of his premises.

'Don't know who you're on about,' Henry Brackenridge insisted in reply to his question regarding the whereabouts of Jack Putnam.

Around them, sides of meat were being loaded onto a cart, and Francis nodded towards the driver, a man he knew as Billy Sneddon. 'Who's he, then?' he asked.

'Billy Sneddon,' Brackenridge replied instantly.

Francis smirked. 'As I thought. A man as notoriously grasping as yourself wouldn't allow a consignment of meat out of here without knowing the identity of the driver, and I have it on good authority that Jack Putnam was seen driving one of your wagons into the marketplace recently. So I ask again, where might I find him?'

'What's he done?' Brackenridge asked sullenly.

Francis employed another common trick that often paid off. 'He's wanted for a most serious crime, for which he could hang.'

'I don't employ murderers,' Brackenridge insisted, 'neither do I hire low types who set fire to houses.'

Francis raised his eyebrows triumphantly. 'I don't recall specifying the hanging offences by name, so thank you for confirming my suspicions. Get word to Jack Putnam that I wish to speak to him about these matters in my room at the Guildhall in the next two days, or it will be *his* house that gets burned down, preferably with him still inside it. Good day,

Alderman Brackenridge, and good luck with your bid to become our next mayor.'

When he got back to their lodgings, Edward was busy filling a borrowed garment bag with just about every item of apparel he owned. He gleefully told Francis that he would be riding north in the company of the Earl of Essex early the following day, in pursuit of Robert Cecil and the kidnapped women. As an added bonus, he would be spending the night somewhere inside Wollaton Hall, and would probably have an opportunity to meet with the enchanting Elizabeth before setting out.

Francis congratulated him, then offered to ride with him as far as the Chapel Bar, where he bid Edward good luck and headed through White Friars, past the castle, and down the Rockyard to The Crusader. A very angry Joan Tanner reminded him, when he enquired after Jack Putnam, that he — Francis — was one of those responsible for her husband Jeb being locked away in the Shire Hall on suspicion of murder. She then ordered him off the premises that she was now attempting to run alone.

Once he arrived back at the Tolney house, Francis slipped from the saddle and tied his horse's bridle to the post, deep in thought. Those who could point the finger in the direction of Jack Putnam were clearly not willing to do so, which further deepened his belief that they were somehow involved. He'd half expected Brackenridge to deny all knowledge of the man, given that their house had been torched and Dickon had been murdered shortly after Edward had made it clear that he knew of Brackenridge's involvement in the poaching of the deer. If the man was intent on keeping his name clear of anything dubious while he made his bid for the office of mayor, then he might have been desperate enough to organise a fire that would put them off the scent while they found somewhere else to live. Francis suspected that the butcher was now panicking that his plans had resulted in murder.

But the reaction of Joan Tanner when he'd enquired about Jack Putnam had come as a complete surprise. Francis had only asked because he'd been informed that Putnam might occasionally work for the Tanners, but her reaction suggested that Putnam's criminal activities on behalf of the proprietors of The Crusader might have been more serious. And hadn't Ellie's body been pulled out of the Leen with a throat so severely cut that only a very sharp knife could have caused the wound? A knife as sharp as the one stolen from Ralph Tolney by Jack Putnam?

So deep in thought was he that he failed to react to the scuffling sound behind him until it was too late. Strong hands gripped him by the throat and begun to squeeze. In vain he elbowed behind him and kicked backwards like an errant horse in its stall, but the hands didn't loosen their grip. He could barely breathe, and the smell of unwashed body was overpowering when he did, so he conserved both his strength and his breath as he continued to buck and kick. Slowly the light that was coming from the mullioned downstairs windows of the Tolney house began to dim before his eyes. He also became aware of a door opening and a man shouting a challenge.

He sank to the ground, then his vision cleared and his throat was no longer in a vicelike grip. He took a few rasping breaths in order to restore air to his lungs as Ralph Tolney lowered his sword and looked anxiously into his eyes.

'A good job I was in the hall awaiting your return so that I could lock up for the night,' Ralph told him. 'That was Jack Putnam, and he would have killed you if I hadn't chased him off!'

12

Edward presented himself at the kitchen door and was curtly told by the cook that supper for the staff was an hour away, and that he would be accommodated in the chamber above the stables. He smiled politely and found where he was to sleep, grateful for the years he'd spent in close proximity to horses. When his rumbling stomach advised him that an hour had probably passed, he went back down to the kitchen, where most of the staff had already assembled for their evening meal.

'You got lucky tonight,' the cook told them all gruffly. 'The lamb that I presented for dinner wasn't entirely eaten, so I gave it to them for their supper as well. There's still some left, so eat it all, because there's no room in the larder for any more leftovers.'

They needed no encouragement, and the chatter ceased abruptly as they ate the remains from the master's table, accompanied by freshly baked black bread and small beer. Edward was just wondering why Elizabeth was not among them when she suddenly appeared in the service doorway that led to the great hall.

'Make way for Beth,' the cook ordered. 'Leave her some of that lamb!'

Elizabeth smiled at Edward as he slid to one side to make room for her on the bench.

'Saves me leaving food out for you for later,' said the cook. 'How come you're here so early in the evening?'

'My mistress has retired early with a sick headache,' Elizabeth explained, 'and little wonder, with the heat in there. The master ordered that the fires be stoked up high, and one can scarcely breathe. It's even hotter than in here, so my mistress began to wilt halfway through the meats. Either that or she was bored by the master's seemingly endless praise of the financial rewards to be obtained from his latest coalmine, which he claims is the latest way to a fortune. If so, then families are condemned to breathe in the foul fumes that are given off when it is burned with such enthusiasm as the master displays. No wonder my mistress was feeling faint, and the Earl of Essex also seemed somewhat incommoded by it. Or perhaps he was as bored as he looked, since he reminded the master more than once that he is destined for an early start on the morrow. With Master Mountsorrel here, it would seem.'

'Indeed, we ride north at daybreak,' Edward confirmed, and all eyes turned to him.

'Why are you riding north?' the cook asked.

'I'm not allowed to disclose that,' he replied simply.

'You're as bad as the men who're riding with the earl,' the cook complained. 'None of them could tell me where they were going or why.'

Elizabeth placed a hot, clammy hand over Edward's. 'I must own that I am still feeling the heat,' she whispered. 'Unless I am to suffer a headache like my mistress, I must go in search of some cool air. Would you be so gracious as to accompany me?'

'I'd be delighted,' Edward replied, 'and I have eaten enough, if you wish to leave now.'

Five minutes later they were back on their customary path. The pale moonlight threw their shadows ahead of them as Elizabeth clung to Edward's arm for support. She looked up and sighed.

'I have missed the sight of stars in the firmament. I always imagine, like the poets tell us, that they are the souls of those who have passed into Heaven. But it seems so long since I have been able to walk like this, underneath their canopy.'

'You are quite the poet yourself,' Edward murmured as he slowed the pace in order to prolong the walk. 'Are you not in the habit of taking the night air of late?'

'Not since I came here. It was fine in my former home, where there was always one of the outdoor workers to accompany me and guard me from harm. But here, as I believe I have already intimated, I am required to be above the company of rough labourers, even for my own safety. And of course there is the ghost of the herdsman who wanders abroad at night.'

'You believe in ghosts?' Edward asked, almost mockingly.

Elizabeth squeezed his arm in mild rebuke. 'It is not just I. Several have seen him out in the deer park — a huge man in wild animal skins, beating through the undergrowth with a long staff, and growling as if searching for quarry.'

'But you have not seen him for yourself?'

'Of course not, since I never venture out here at night. You have no idea how comforting it is to have you so close beside me.'

To emphasise her point, she pulled him closer. Just then, there was a loud screeching from the trees that overhung the shrubbery, and Elizabeth gave a frightened squawk and threw herself into Edward's arms. He held her tightly for a moment, savouring the warmth of her body and her rich perfume before laughing lightly and pushing her a little away from him in order to look into her eyes.

'It was you, during a previous walk in this place, who bid me speak plainly. You, like myself, were raised in the country, and could not possibly have mistaken the screech of an owl for anything else. If you wanted me to embrace you warmly, you only had to ask.'

'Embrace me warmly,' she said coquettishly, 'for I am discovered. As your reward, you may kiss me on the lips.'

Their lips locked urgently and longingly before Elizabeth pushed Edward gently away.

'I now appreciate what they say about how easy it is to fall into carnal sin,' she said. 'It is as well that I am accommodated in the side chamber to my mistress's, while you reside temporarily among the smell of horses. But it will not always be that way, so please come back alive from whatever your business may be with the Earl of Essex.'

Francis was assuring Emma Tolney for the fifth time that he was none the worse for being strangled, while Ralph was reminding him that Putnam had clearly intended to kill him. He pointed to the deep red weals on his neck.

'They will be gone before morning,' Francis assured him, 'but my fear is for your good selves. This is a man who did not shrink from setting fire to our house, remember. Who is to say that he will not return and do likewise to yours, with us in it? I must redouble my efforts to hunt Putnam down, and place him where he can be of no danger to anyone else.'

'I trust that you will not venture to do so alone?' Ralph asked.

'As part of my duties I have command of the town constables, and they are a sturdy crew of men. I shall ensure that I am in the company of at least two of them wherever I wander during the daylight hours, and once it is dark I shall again impose upon your hospitality.'

'It's no imposition,' Emma assured him. 'In fact, in these Godless times it's good to have a law officer such as yourself under our roof.'

'Not when he is being sought by a lunatic who has probably killed twice already,' Francis said ruefully as he once again drew a soothing hand over the deep red welts on his neck.

The following morning Francis lost no time in trotting his horse down to the Guildhall and summoning Constables Draycott and Eames from their room to accompany him on his rounds of the town streets. They began on the east side, then headed north along the remains of the old town wall that these days would barely prove resistant to even a flock of sheep. They then crossed to the north side of the town proper along Coalpit Lane before heading back south through the marketplace and down into Whitefriars Lane, where the remains of the old house had been largely rebuilt using the latest building material, bricks fired in the kilns of Mapperley Plains to the north, from where suitable clay could be dug. The traditional roof thatch had been forsworn by the town authorities when commissioning the new house, and Francis gazed in fascination at the roof tiles that were being hammered into place along the newly erected roof timbers. His former neighbour, Josiah Thrumpton, sidled up to him as he stood with his horse's bridle in his hand.

'Will you be coming back soon?' Josiah asked. 'Only the missus will be mightily relieved to have you back in our midst for our protection.'

Francis laughed sourly. 'Take a look at what is happening there, Josiah. My house is being rebuilt because I was unable to protect it from the schemes of a villain. So how might I protect you from the same?'

'You never caught the man responsible?' Josiah asked hesitantly, and when Francis shook his head, Josiah looked sheepish. 'I might've caught him for you, had I realised what he were about.'

'Your meaning?' Francis asked.

'Well, you'll recall how we never put fences up between our rear gardens, and my dog Rufus used to go ratting in your cabbage patch?'

'Yes, so what?'

'Well, the night your house burned down, I heard him barking fit to burst. I rushed out before the neighbours on the other side could complain, and there he was.'

'Who?' Francis demanded, wondering how a man of such few words could earn a living as a sign writer.

'The man who set fire to your house — at least, I think it was him. The place went up just after that, only Rufus had the man by the hand, and wouldn't let go. I was daft enough to call him off — not realising what the man had just done, you understand — and he ran off. He must have been pretty sore in the hand, because Rufus still had bits of blood and skin in his mouth when he come back to the house, looking right pleased with himself.'

'So if I've got this right,' Francis replied, 'there was a man in your back garden shortly before our house went up in flames, and your dog bit him severely on the hand before he escaped. Why did you call the dog off?'

'Because there have been complaints that he's bitten other folk who come near our house, and I didn't want the constables coming to take him away. He's normally a good dog, when I'm there to tell him what to do.'

'But this man — you didn't recognise him?'

'No, it was dark, and I was more concerned that Rufus might chew him up if I didn't call him off.'

'But whoever it was might still have an injured hand?'

'Maybe. Like I said, Rufus took quite a chunk out of it.'

'Thank you very much, Josiah. Rest assured that I won't be reporting your dog for his behaviour, provided that you keep him tied up in future.'

'Thanks, Master Barton. And the sooner you get back here, the easier me and Maggie will be able to rest at night.'

Francis rejoined his colleagues, realising that whoever had gripped him so fiercely by the throat the previous evening had not been suffering a hand injury. Perhaps he'd been too eager to pin Dickon's death and the torching of the house on Jack Putnam, but the fact remained that the knife that had been used to kill poor Dickon had been stolen in the first place by Putnam, so he must have either sold or loaned it to somebody. And that dreadful double crime followed hard on Edward's questioning of Henry Brackenridge regarding stolen venison, so there was an obvious further enquiry to be made in that quarter.

Francis ordered his two constables back up Whitefriars Lane and into Timber Hill, then instructed them to accompany him to the butchery yard, where Brackenridge was supervising the pouring of buckets of water onto the cobbles, which were still streaked with animal blood. Francis walked straight up to Brackenridge and ordered him to hold out both hands. Brackenridge went pale as he did as instructed.

Francis took a firm hold of the healing scar on Brackenridge's left hand, then turned to his constables. 'Take him away, lads.'

'What for?' Brackenridge demanded.

Francis grabbed him by the tunic front. 'The murder of Richard Keyworth, who was worth ten times more than you! He would never have been made Mayor of Nottingham, but neither will you now!'

13

'How many days' ride away is the place in York of which you spoke?' Edward asked Essex breathlessly as they galloped past Bestwood Lodge the next morning.

'That depends upon the speed and stamina of your horse, does it not?' said Essex. 'And the amount of breath that you have available when you have finished asking questions.'

Edward took the hint and remained silent as he watched the familiar fields and hedgerows flash past. Behind them thundered four mounted soldiers wearing the Essex livery, and at this pace Edward estimated that they would reach Rufford Abbey by mid-morning at the latest. From there they might perhaps command a change of horse, and be at Sheffield Manor in the late afternoon, if not earlier.

When they arrived at Rufford Abbey, they stayed for long enough to drink some small beer and answer calls of nature. They then pounded along the North Road as the fields of Nottinghamshire gave way to the rolling slopes of South Yorkshire. The sun was just beyond its highest point when they cantered into the courtyard of Sheffield Manor, and grooms ran out to take their horses by the bridle. The slim, elegant, black-bearded George Talbot, Seventh Earl of Shrewsbury, emerged through the front door. His regular, if not frequent, attendances at court enabled him to recognise his visitor.

'My Lord of Essex?' he asked in disbelief.

Essex confirmed his identity. 'I am advised that Master Robert Cecil was a guest here not many days ago — is that correct?'

'Indeed he was,' Talbot said nervously. 'He claimed to be on Her Majesty's business, and given the esteem with which his worthy father was once regarded by that most gracious of ladies...'

'Tell me how many days since, Talbot. And where was he bound?'

'It would have been Sunday when he departed, having been here for two nights. He was bound, or so he said, for Selby, and from thence to York. Was I wrong to offer my humble hospitality?'

'No, fear not,' Essex assured him. 'But hopefully that same hospitality may now be offered to myself and my party. We require dinner, somewhere to wash the dust from our clothing, gallons of small beer and a complete change of horses. You may expect us back within the week in order to retrieve our own, which we leave to the good offices of your grooms, who will hopefully treat them with kindness.'

'Rest assured, that may all be provided,' Talbot replied, visibly relieved. 'I shall give immediate instruction to the cook to set about preparing a late dinner, and in the meantime you might like to refresh yourselves indoors. I shall have beer sent into the great hall immediately, and the washerwoman will see to the cleaning of such clothes as you may wish to leave with us until your return.'

An hour later, dressed in fresh clothes and halfway through their third jug of beer, Essex smiled across the oak table at Edward. 'Do you wonder why I am seemingly so anxious to rescue five prostitutes?'

'Indeed, my lord, it has puzzled me that you were so ready to espouse their cause. Would it be impertinent of me to suggest that it perhaps owes more to your concern that the image of

Her Majesty would be sullied in the eyes of those who grace the Scottish court?'

Essex laughed lightly, then fixed Edward with a hard stare. 'May I rely upon you to say nothing to anyone of what I am about to reveal to you?'

'You may,' Edward replied firmly. 'Do you wish me to swear an oath to that effect?'

'No, simply listen, and do not repeat what you hear. First, might I ask what you know of matters at court?'

'Virtually nothing, my lord. I am aware that the beautiful and triumphant Elizabeth Tudor is our monarch, that she grows graciously into her middle years, and that for most of her reign she relied on the counsel of the father of Robert Cecil.'

Essex nodded condescendingly. 'With such honeyed words, you might survive for some time at court, until the wrong word sent you to the block. Be advised that Elizabeth fears enemies on all sides, from all elements of her subjects, and even within the walls of her several palaces. This makes her mightily suspicious of anything that smacks of sedition, or any form of challenge to her throne.'

'I have heard something of these matters,' Edward replied, 'although this has only been through the idle chatter that drifts down through busy tongues after it has been harvested by keen ears at the serving table, or in the hunting parks.'

'Then you must also have heard that Elizabeth lacks an heir?'

'That she remains unmarried, certainly. I had the privilege of serving under your esteemed stepfather the Earl of Leicester at Tilbury, where we stood to arms against the Spanish threat. It was rumoured among the soldiers there — and forgive me if I speak out of turn — that there was once a possibility that Leicester might become husband to Her Majesty.'

'Indeed, there was a time when even he believed this,' Essex smiled wryly, 'but when that opportunity passed, he became greatly enamoured of my mother, much to Elizabeth's displeasure. But therein lies another history altogether. For whatever reason, England will want for a monarch if Elizabeth dies tomorrow.'

'But surely...' Edward began.

Essex raised a hand to silence him. 'I do not say that she will, so do not interpret those words as a prediction of her death, else it will be my head on the block. I say merely that as matters stand, there is no immediate and obvious Tudor heir.'

'Can Her Majesty not appoint her own heir?'

'There is indeed a fairly recent precedent for such, but it nearly led to a civil war. When King Edward VI died, he devolved the Crown upon a distant cousin, Jane Grey of Bradgate, whose mother was a niece to his father, the eighth Henry. But Henry had previously provided for the next in line to be his natural daughter Mary, which left the nation in uproar. This must never happen again, and Her Majesty is very conscious of the need to avoid chaos following her death. But she does not see her death as imminent.'

'And is it?'

A look of horror spread over Essex's face. 'One must never speak of the death of a monarch, because it is deemed treasonous. This is why we must take care when seeking to advise Elizabeth of the need to proclaim an heir to her throne, because she is wont to regard such talk as encompassing her death.'

'So what is to be done?' Edward asked.

Essex sighed. 'Now you come to the nub of it. There are two possible lines of succession, both from sisters of Henry VIII. His older sister Margaret first married the Scottish King James, but after his death she became the Countess of Lennox. She in turn had two sons, the older of whom was Lord Darnley, father of the current King of Scotland, James VI. There is considerable support at court for his claim, but Elizabeth had his Catholic mother, Mary Stuart, executed, which was partly the cause of her excommunication by the Pope and the justification for the failed Spanish invasion. Elizabeth therefore fears that leaving her crown to James will reopen the door to Catholicism within her kingdom, and she dares not have that upon her dying conscience. James makes much of being a Protestant, but Catholic hopes within the nation rest upon his becoming our next monarch and respecting his late mother's religion. Those hopes are being fanned in secret by Cecil and his son, who nevertheless regard James as the only hope for their own Protestant faith to continue as the national religion.'

'Which is why Robert Cecil is riding north?'

'Precisely. The Cecils are of the firm belief that James of Scotland will become James of England, and they curry favour with him in the hope of high office following his coronation. Robert in particular burns with resentment of his ridicule at court, and of Elizabeth's demeaning behaviour towards him. You will of course be aware of the sensitivity of men who lack height in this world of ours, in which being tall is regarded as essential if one is to progress and aspire to high office.'

'But there are other potential heirs to Elizabeth, you say?'

'There is one only, but she is a staunch and unrepentant Catholic. The Countess of Lennox had a younger son, and his daughter, Arbella Stuart, has almost an equal claim to that of James. Her grandfather was the previous Earl of Shrewsbury — so the man who will be providing our dinner this day is her great uncle. Talbot lives in hope that she will become Queen Arbella, thus raising the family's diminishing fortunes, and no doubt Robert Cecil fed upon his ambition when imposing his party upon his hospitality. Such is the treacherous nature of the Cecils that for some years they let it be believed that they supported Arbella's claim to the throne, all the while seeking the good opinions of James of Scotland.'

Edward shook his head in an effort to clear his thoughts. 'It is as well that I did not choose the courtly life, for my head swims with all this information. But I believe that I now understand why Robert Cecil is taking James the gift of prostitutes. He must be a lustful man indeed.'

'Not James himself,' Essex replied. 'James likes to appear as the very model of marital fidelity towards his new wife, Anne of Denmark. In this regard his court at Edinburgh is said to be the last word in moral chastity, although there are those who claim — privately, of course — that James's preference runs towards handsome young men. But at Stirling it is a different story altogether.'

'And that is where the women are destined to go?'

'So I believe. The court moves regularly to Stirling, where it is out of sight of the joyless Presbyterian faction that helps to support James on his throne. At Stirling they compensate for their chastity in Edinburgh with all manner of depravity, in which the women are no doubt intended to be unwilling participants.'

'How do you know these things?' Edward asked, horrified.

'Cecil is not the only one with his fingers in two pies at once. I need to keep one step ahead of him if I am to persuade Her Majesty that I should be entrusted with an army to march north and remind the King of Scotland that his mother was treasonous, that his court is a moral cesspit, and that he is not fit to ascend to the throne of England. But Elizabeth fears to engage in such fashion, lest those who remain loyal to the memory of Mary Stuart foment a Catholic rebellion. This is why she merely smiles at the regular congress between the Cecils and the Scots court, in the belief that they are negotiating a lasting peace, when in fact they are worming away at her succession.'

'Would she be likely to react badly, were she to learn of this underhand behaviour on the part of those in whom she most trusts?' Edward asked.

Essex nodded. 'She might well never trust either of them ever again, given her unforgiving and suspicious nature these days. This is when she will hopefully realise that she may trust in me.'

Whatever the earl's motives, Edward knew he would not have got this far without his support, and he was anxious to harness it further. 'How may I assist in this venture?' he asked.

The answer came suspiciously quickly. 'You must be my ears and eyes, Edward. You may easily mingle among those of lesser status, such as stable hands. When dinner is served, eat swiftly and take yourself off to the stables, with the excuse of seeing to the saddling of our new mounts. Ask how Cecil was able to hide the abduction of the women from our host — if indeed he did — while I keep the ambitious old fool in idle conversation regarding recent affairs at court. Report to me all you have learned tonight, when hopefully we'll reach Selby before darkness descends upon our track.'

'You believe that we can reach Selby before nightfall?'

'I know that I can,' said Essex. 'Let us hope that you are at least half the man you appear to be, and that these borrowed horses are equal to the challenge. If not, then we are destined to spend the night in some pestilential inn along the way.'

14

Edward and Essex managed to ride as far as the village of Askern before they agreed that the horses were likely to expire under them if they didn't halt for the night. A surly innkeeper adopted a different tone when he saw the colour of Essex's money, and learned his name and the nature of his business. After a hasty meal of cold cuts and slightly stale bread, washed down with local ale, they fell eagerly onto the straw pallets in their shared room. Their four-man escort was accommodated in the stables in which the horses were rubbed down and fed by a grumpy ostler.

The following morning was cold and clear, and they took their time over breakfast when told that Cawood Castle was only a half day's ride further north.

'Tell me what you learned back in Sheffield regarding how Cecil managed to conceal his captives, assuming that he managed to keep them alive,' Essex demanded.

Edward frowned. 'That must indeed have been a miracle, but as Nottingham prostitutes they are accustomed to rough living. The stable hands at Sheffield Manor spoke of them in tones of bewilderment. Once the main party had been ushered into the house, the few men at arms who accompanied the party unfurled the litters and carried five women into the barn, where they were laid down in some straw in the groom's quarters, awoken from what appeared to be a drunken slumber, and fed for the night. The stable hands were ordered away, and a screen was erected in front of where the women lay. Then the following morning they were carried back into the litters, after those watching were advised that the ladies had consumed too much wine the previous night.'

'And they believed that pigswill?'

'So it would seem, although they claimed never to have seen anything like it before. They all commented that if they were indeed ladies, they were poorly dressed and filthy.'

'We must assume that the same scheme will be employed at York,' Essex mused, 'although we must hope that the poison they are being fed to keep them silent does not prove to be their demise.'

'I was wondering about that, too,' said Edward. 'How do you think they have been kept alive?'

Essex shrugged. 'Cecil is known for his fixation on physicians, who have tended to him for most of his life. He may have one in his travelling entourage. Either that or a skilled apothecary supplied him with sufficient potion to last him until he reaches Stirling. Even so, he must be growing anxious, and this is likely to oblige him to cut short his time in York.'

'Will we overtake him there?'

'We shall perhaps know better when we reach Cawood. And now, if you have eaten sufficient, we must lose no time in doing so.'

Later that morning, as they trotted slowly down the long slope towards the gatehouse of Cawood Castle, Edward asked about the elegant spires he could see in the far distance, and was told that they belonged to York Minster.

'The place where we are destined to spend the night was once the official residence of the Archbishops of York,' Essex told him. 'It was as close as Cardinal Wolsey ever got to his official duties in that role, before being hauled back to London on a charge of treason, dying on the way. Once Henry

143

completed his robbery of every former holy house in the name of Protestantism, this noble pile became a royal residence, and it still is. Since it is owned by the Crown, it is maintained for the convenience and comfort of all who ride on the queen's business. No doubt Cecil made use of that only a few nights since.'

'Why, then, would he choose to move on to York, which appears to be only an hour or so to our north?' Edward asked.

Essex snorted derisively. 'Did I not advise you that Master Robert Cecil enjoys his creature comforts? This large edifice that we are about to enter has, they say, been allowed to fall into some disrepair, and you will no doubt experience its lack of comfort before we smoke out Cecil in his lair at Manor Lodge, which has much more to offer the weary traveller or the devious schemer. But Cawood was once good enough for the prelates of the true faith; therefore, it will suffice for me.'

Edward tucked more information into his head as they dismounted. It would seem that Essex harboured secret Catholic beliefs. Given his attempts to thwart Cecil in his communications with James of Scotland, it seemed that he might favour the claim of the other possible heir to the throne, Arbella Stuart. But Edward was grateful to Essex for assisting him this far, so he held his tongue.

The steward of Cawood appeared to be the most senior man entrusted with the maintenance of this once elegant, but now sadly neglected, royal residence. He was only too happy to advise Essex and Edward that Robert Cecil and his party had spent only one night there before moving on to York, although he did not know where in York they might have taken up temporary residence. When Edward enquired if Cecil's party had contained any women, the man grew visibly nervous and replied that he had no personal knowledge of any. However, he had been advised by the cook that meals had been taken out to the courtyard by several of Cecil's men, who had then returned and demanded food for themselves. The party had left two days previously, before noon.

The following morning, Edward and Essex mounted their horses, now confident that they would catch up with Cecil.

'We have him!' Essex muttered gleefully as they trotted into the forecourt of King's Manor and saw three closed litters abandoned down one side of the cobbled yard, with the stable doors on the other. Several stable boys ran to take their horses' bridles as they dismounted, and Essex handed one of them a coin.

'This is for you, if you can tell me where I might find the ladies who arrived in those litters two days since.'

The lad looked almost disbelievingly at the coin in his hand, greater in value than a month's wages. He then pointed eagerly behind him to a closed door to the right of the main stable door.

'They're in there, good sir, but they don't seem to be in the mood for anything but sleeping. Sir Richard said that they were to be left undisturbed. Food is taken to them from time to time, but they haven't been out of there since they were first led in. I think they were drunk.'

'There is a good reason for that,' Essex replied grimly as he beckoned for Edward to accompany him towards the door in question, then turned back to the stable boy. 'Inform this Sir Richard that I require his presence here now,' he demanded.

'It's not my place, sir,' the lad replied, 'but I'll tell the steward, and he'll pass on your instruction.'

The door offered no resistance when Edward pushed it open with his boot, and he and Essex stepped slowly into the darkness beyond. The smell of unwashed bodies was overpowering, and they both gagged. This, together with the light that they had admitted into the gloom, seemed to rouse someone. A pale hand appeared from behind a straw bale. 'Is it time for us to be fed again?' a weak voice asked.

Edward stepped back two paces and threw the doors wide open. Light streamed in, revealing the comatose forms of five women, separated from each other by bales of straw. One of them sat up, rubbed her eyes, squinted at the two intruders and demanded, 'Where's Richard?'

'Is one of you Nell Franklin?' Edward asked gently.

The woman gestured behind her. 'She's back there, but I'm Annie. Is Richard on his way with some food for us? We're all thirsty as well.'

'We're here to secure your release,' Edward explained as tactfully as he could, and a faint cheer could be heard from another woman somewhere near the back. It was followed almost immediately by a bellow from a male voice in the open doorway behind them.

'Who are you, and what's your business here?'

Essex and Edward turned. Behind them stood a tall man wearing a feathered bonnet, with his hands on his hips. Essex drew his sword and advanced on the man, Edward following closely behind him. Their interrogator looked to be in his thirties, with a well-manicured black beard and clear brown eyes. He was elegantly dressed for someone who had presumably been on the road as part of Cecil's entourage. His blue tunic was slashed with silver in the new fashion, and he had a dark brown cape slung over one shoulder in the Spanish style.

'I am Robert Devereux, Earl of Essex. I am here to rescue these ladies,' Essex announced haughtily. 'This gentleman with me is Edward Mountsorrel, bailiff to the Sheriff of

Nottinghamshire, the county from which these unfortunate women were abducted and thrown into the baggage train of Master Robert Cecil, whom I presume you serve? If that be the case, tell him that I am here in the queen's name, demanding an explanation for such vile and treasonous behaviour.'

'How "treasonous"?' the man demanded.

'They are being conveyed to the Scottish court at Stirling, are they not, where they are to be defiled as a present from Her Majesty Queen Elizabeth? The disgrace that such traffic would bring down upon her name is so onerous as to be treasonable. However, whether or not I report this to Her Majesty on my return to London will depend upon the attitude displayed by Master Cecil. You might wish to inform him that we are here, and await his presence at this scene of wickedness and depravity.'

Edward walked a few paces back into the barn and looked down at Annie. 'Annie Freebourne?' he asked.

She nodded. 'Yes — where are we this time?'

'York, on the way to Scotland. Do you know that man in the doorway wearing the bonnet?'

'Yes,' Annie spat. 'He's Richard, the evil bastard what led to us all being kidnapped. But you've come to take us home, you said?'

Edward was about to assure her that this was the case when Richard turned and ran. Edward gave a shout and raced after him at top speed, executing a flying dive halfway toward the open front doors to King's Manor that brought them both to the cobbles in a cloud of dust. Fists began to fly as Edward uttered one foul oath after another, while men at arms from Essex's retinue surrounded the pair, yelling encouragement to Edward, who was clearly winning the fight. However, a strong hand yanked him off his adversary by the collar of his tunic, while another hand put a sword tip to Richard's throat.

'Don't kill him now,' Essex told the swordsman. 'Save him for the hangman.'

'What is this outrage?' came a reedy voice from the entrance to King's Manor. 'Who dares to brawl in my presence?' Cecil strode across to the group and looked challengingly down at Edward as he was rising to his feet, dusting down his doublet and hose. Cecil's gaze then transferred to Essex, and his mouth dropped open.

'You!' he yelled. 'What devil's work brings *you* here?'

'The devilry that you are engaged in,' Essex snarled back. 'Did Her Majesty direct you to transfer prostitutes from Nottingham to Stirling?'

'I travel to Edinburgh on her business, certainly,' Cecil replied evasively, 'bearing dispatches from my father.'

'And the prostitutes?' Essex repeated. 'Did your father order you to collect those on your travels?'

'I know not to what you refer,' Cecil defied him.

Essex turned to point at Edward. 'This man carries the authority of the Sheriff of Nottinghamshire, and he is here to return to their homes those women whom one in your party kidnapped and brought north. You cannot claim ignorance of the three closed litters containing young women who have spent almost a week drugged into insensibility. I hazard a guess that they were destined to be delivered to the Scottish court at Stirling, and that Her Majesty remains ignorant of your scheme. As to whether or not your father was privy to it will remain unknown until I speak to him.'

The wind seemed to have been taken from Cecil's sails as he asked, 'What business took you to Nottingham?'

'A request from Her Majesty that I inspect the new mansion at Wollaton that has been constructed in her honour by Sir Francis Willoughby, which he is desirous that she visit. While there, I was informed by this worthy gentleman, Edward Mountsorrel, of the wicked deeds of this cur whom Mountsorrel would have killed had I not stayed his hand. He will no doubt be more than happy to advise us whence came his orders once we have him in the Tower, and he is put to the question employing certain processes designed to elicit the truth.'

'Master!' the man on the ground pleaded. 'Tell him that I only did as directed, in the belief that it was the queen's wish!'

Cecil looked guiltily across at Essex and gave a crooked smile. 'Come inside, Robert, and let us take some wine together while we discuss this matter.'

Essex looked sideways at Edward. 'If I leave you to seek further information from this man who calls himself Richard, do I have your word that you will not kill him?'

'You do,' Edward replied, 'but I give you no guarantee that he will be capable of walking once I have finished obtaining that further information.'

Essex smiled. 'He will not be required to walk anyway, with his hands and feet bound, and seated backwards on a pack horse. I shall send for a physician who can advise us whether these women are in a fit condition to make the journey home. Then we shall decide whether Richard here is to be taken to Nottingham for execution, or to the Tower for further interrogation. That may well depend on how forthcoming Master Cecil proves to be. Join us for refreshment once you have the answers you need.'

On Edward's orders, Richard was hauled to his feet and manhandled into the barn that contained the women. He was tied with his wrists suspended from a roof beam, then the rope was hauled tight enough to ensure that he was obliged to remain on tiptoe in order to minimise the strain on his arms.

The women were beginning to come round, and they gathered in a group, jeering, spitting and cat-calling in front of where Richard was all but hanging by his arms. Edward instructed them all to be seated.

'You may enjoy what is to follow, and advise me if this wretch attempts to tell me a single lie,' he said.

'What do you want to know?' the man asked as he winced with the effort of remaining on his toes.

'We'll begin with your name,' Edward demanded.

'Richard Winfield.'

'Not "*Sir* Richard", then?' one of the women called.

He shook his head as Edward raised a hand for silence, then demanded, 'How did you get involved in all this?'

'I was promised a military commission,' Winfield explained. 'I was one of the men at arms at Whitehall Palace, and I was assigned to ensuring the safety of Secretary Cecil, Robert Cecil's father. When we came north I was attached to Robert Cecil's bodyguard, and he promised that if I could bring about the queen's wish that women be taken north to curry favour with the King of Scotland, then she could be persuaded to give me a commission in her army in Ireland.'

He paused, panting, and Edward allowed him a short respite while the women continued to hurl obscenities at him.

'You drugged the women inside The Crusader, then had them conveyed into the passageway inside the castle rock, did you not?' he asked.

Winfield nodded.

'How did you know that this would be possible, and who assisted you?'

'Cecil told me to speak in secret with the man who ran the inn, and he said that the commanding officer of the castle garrison had agreed for the women to be handed over to him. I was told about the door behind the cupboard, and I was to let the innkeeper know when there was a woman ready to be taken out through that door, and he'd do the rest. I assumed that they were taken away through there, but I never got involved in that, I swear. Can you let me lower my arms for just a moment, please?'

'Let the cur suffer!' one of the women yelled, but Edward ordered that the rope be slackened.

'The bastard will talk more easily if he's not struggling for breath,' he said. 'Trust me, he'll get what's coming to him.'

'Just let us at him, and we'll rip him apart!' shouted another woman, to be met by rousing cheers.

'Please!' Winfield whispered to Edward as his face contorted in fear.

Edward decided to push on while he had the man at such a disadvantage. 'So Colonel Waldegrave from the castle was in on it too, was he?'

'He must have been, because the women were always whisked away as soon as I sent word to the innkeeper — a man called Tanner, as I recall.'

'That's him,' Edward confirmed. 'But who else was in on this wicked scheme of yours?'

'Nobody — and it wasn't really my scheme,' Winfield objected. 'By the time I was talked into it by Cecil, who assured me that I was just the man for the job with my good looks and courtly bearing, it seemed that everything else had been organised.'

151

'And there were only these five women here?' Edward asked. 'There were none who died in the process of being drugged, or who were left behind?'

'There were just these five, and I only put a small amount of the powder into their drinks.'

'For all you knew, you were poisoning them to death!' Edward shouted.

'It was merely valerian, which I have myself sometimes taken as a sleeping draught, and it may be obtained from any apothecary,' Winfield said quickly. 'It was required for long enough to keep the women quiescent while they were being held. It is particularly effective when mixed with a heavy wine, which also serves to mask its unusual odour.'

'We could have died, you bastard!' Annie yelled. 'I'll put _you_ to sleep for good, when I get my hands on you!'

The colour drained from Winfield's face. 'You wouldn't?'

Edward shook his head. 'You have to hope that I don't change my mind, though, don't you? I could leave you tied up and defenceless while these women show you the same mercy that you showed them. You're lucky there are only five of them. Was that all you were told to collect, or did something happen to make you call a halt to the scheme?'

Winfield nodded. 'There would have been more, but I lost my nerve after the one who died.'

'You previously denied any knowledge of a dead woman!' Edward said sharply. 'What happened to her — did you overdo the valerian?'

'No, nothing like that,' Winfield hastened to assure him as he cast a fearful look towards the group of women. 'In fact, she wasn't one of my marks at all — just another woman whom Tanner had obviously singled out for himself, and had killed in the process. I was just leaving The Crusader after what turned

152

out to be the final woman was sent into that tunnel under the castle, and as I went through to the barrel store at the back, there was a woman lying there with her throat cut. Tanner was struggling to get her out of sight, and he asked me to lend him a hand to get rid of the body. I refused and we had a short argument. He told me that I was useless, but that he knew somebody with a barrow who could help him, so I got out of there as fast as I could and went back to where I was lodging with Master Cecil in the town.'

'Did Tanner say who this man with the barrow was?' Edward asked.

'He only said that he knew someone. I wasn't anxious to remain there any longer, what with the dead woman and all that blood.'

Edward nodded to the man who had control of the rope. 'You can let him down now,' he said. 'I'll take him into the main house, if only for his own safety. See to it that these ladies are fed and watered, and cleaned up as far as possible before they're examined by the physician.'

'What will you tell Her Majesty?' Cecil demanded, clearly nervous but anxious to maintain as much dignity as he could.

Essex smiled sadistically. 'I will probably tell her nothing, if only to preserve your scrawny neck. But remember my charity the next time you're thinking of opposing me. I will, however, probably advise your father, in order that he may be made aware of how little you can be trusted to carry out his simple commissions. Or was the idea his in the first place?'

'It was all mine, I assure you,' Cecil conceded, 'and my father will berate me fiercely when he learns of what has happened. Not for what I did, I suspect, because it was upon his instruction that I was seeking to ingratiate myself with King

James. But he will be angered that I was caught out — particularly by you. Must I now abandon my journey north?'

'I see no reason why you should. For one thing, the further away from court you are, the happier am I. Secondly, I respect your father's powers of intrigue and statesmanship. If he believes that it is in England's best interests to appease the Scottish king, then I must assume that it is. But clearly I shall be taking your prisoners back to their homes.'

'What about Master Winfield?'

Essex thought for a moment. 'I would dearly like to take him down to London and have him hanged, but I would need some justification for that, even in these fraught and suspicious times. The same goes for the commander of the garrison back in Nottingham, who should by rights be deprived of his office. But in either case I would need to reveal the full depth of your infamy to Her Majesty, whereas it suits my purpose to leave you hanging by the thread of fear.'

'You are a double-dyed bastard, Essex, as I have always maintained.'

'I thank you for your compliment,' Essex said with a smirk, 'since it takes one to know one. As we are both fully aware, it is the only way to survive at court.'

Essex faced a much harder task in persuading Edward that they would simply be taking the women back to Nottingham, and nothing more. Edward was at first disbelieving, and then he expressed his concerns loudly as they sat enjoying a late dinner that Cecil had declined to share with them. He had withdrawn to his upper chamber, the door to which was guarded by one of Essex's armed men.

'But what of those who should be brought to justice?' Edward protested. 'That low villain Winfield, Colonel Waldegrave, and the innkeeper Tanner, not to mention Cecil himself?'

Essex sighed. 'It is time that you learned something of the realities of life at the court of Elizabeth of England, Edward. There may come a time when Cecil is exposed for the devious rat that he is, but it suits me to await a suitable moment. His wings will be sufficiently clipped when his more intelligent father learns of the disgrace that his son has brought upon the family name. Baron Burghley is still well regarded by Her Majesty, even though he is currently banished from court. He is well placed to save his son's neck from the block unless and until I can prove him guilty of something more directly and clearly treasonous. As matters stand, he is merely revealed as a slimy fool who cannot be trusted with a simple errand. You must look elsewhere for your scapegoat, although upon my return to London I will find some grounds upon which to have the castle commander stripped of his office. But you sought my assistance to rescue the Nottingham women, and you have achieved this.'

'What would happen were I to reveal all that I have learned?' Edward asked.

Essex smiled unpleasantly. 'The County of Nottinghamshire would be in urgent need of a new sheriff's bailiff.'

'You would have me killed?'

'Not directly. I would simply report to Her Majesty that you sought to thwart England's efforts to maintain peaceful relations with our traditional enemies north of the border.'

'You would tell a lie, when I could prove it to be such?'

'And who would believe you and a handful of local prostitutes, against the word of Her Majesty's rapidly rising favourite? In which capacity I am able to return the favour you have granted me in putting Cecil on the back foot.'

'In what way?'

'Before we set off from Wollaton Hall, I was approached by a delightfully comely young lady by the name of Elizabeth. I do not recall the other name she supplied, but she is seemingly employed in the Willoughby household.'

'You speak of Elizabeth Porter, the lady who attends the daughter of the family?'

'I believe that to be her. She pleaded most ardently with me to bring you back safely, from which I deduce that you are important to her, and perhaps she to you?'

'And what of it?'

'She also asked that I speak highly of you to Sir Francis, in order that he might look favourably upon regular visits by you to Wollaton. I could tell for myself, upon our first meeting, that he does not approve of you for some reason. Whatever that reason, I believe that I may be able to restore your good name in his eyes, in return for your silence.'

'You would give a good report to him of my recent actions?' Edward replied sceptically. 'How could you do that without revealing what we have both learned this past few days?'

'That is not what I had in mind. Sir Francis would give his right arm to have Her Majesty visit his magnificent residence. I believe I might prevail upon her to do so once the next spring is upon us, and she is minded to move her court around the country. I could then let it be believed by Sir Francis that I so persuaded her upon your urging.'

'You would do me such a service?'

'I would be more than happy to do so, in return for your continued discretion regarding the service you have rendered me.'

Edward smiled. 'I believe I have learned my first lesson in courtly intrigue. And I can at least bring one man to justice for what went on inside The Crusader.'

15

There was no mistaking the summons that landed on his desk inside the Guildhall, and Francis sighed with irritation. He normally met with Sheriff Freeman on Monday mornings, and this morning was a Friday. The matter was obviously urgent, and Francis had a horrible suspicion that he knew what it was. He was not mistaken.

He'd barely made it inside the front hall of the sheriff's spacious house on Stoney Street when the imperious voice of his employer boomed out from the sitting room to the rear of the ground floor.

'If that's Barton, get yourself in here now!'

Francis braced himself for the verbal spray that was Freeman's principal way of expressing his displeasure, and he did not have long to wait. He had barely appeared in the doorway when the question was asked.

'What in God's name possessed you to arrest Alderman Brackenridge?'

'Suspicion of arson and murder, sir.'

'Of what, and whom?'

'Our house in Whitefriars Lane, and Dickon — Richard Keyworth — our servant.'

'You are accusing one of the town's leading members of such heinous crimes? What is your evidence?'

'He was identified as being at the scene at the time, sir. By my neighbour.'

'Your neighbour being?'

'Josiah Thrumpton, the sign writer.'

'Is that all? And didn't this all occur during the dead of night? So, a fleeting glimpse of a man in darkness — is that all the evidence you have?'

'There's more than that,' Francis insisted, already beginning to bristle with anger. 'The person responsible was attacked by Thrumpton's dog, which hung on to his hand and took a lump out of it. When I called on Brackenridge after learning that, he had an injury to his hand that he couldn't explain.'

'Did you ask him to?'

'No, as it happens. The look on his face spoke loudly of his guilt.'

'So you expect me to present the alderman for trial on charges that carry death as a punishment simply because of a coincidence that you didn't bother to investigate properly?'

'The knife that killed Dickon — Master Keyworth — when he tried to prevent the setting of the fire was stolen from the house of Ralph Tolney, where I am currently abiding. The thief was Jack Putnam, who used to conduct labouring work for him.'

'So have you arrested this Putnam?'

'He's gone into hiding, sir, but we've put the word out for him.'

'But if Putnam stole the knife, why have you charged Alderman Brackenridge?'

'Putnam also worked occasionally for Brackenridge, and may well have sold him the knife.'

'And that's it — that's all you have, bearing in mind that this Putnam could have sold, or even loaned, the knife to anyone?'

'I suggest that the coincidences are simply too many, sir. Enough for a jury to bring in a true bill.'

'You know as well as I, Barton, that a petty Nottingham jury would find a true bill against their own grandmothers for high treason if it was time for their suppers. Then we're left looking like total fools when the grand jury finds the man not guilty.'

'That's a risk we take in all cases, sir.'

'But not a risk I'm prepared to take in respect of the man who is favoured to become our next mayor. I want Alderman Brackenridge released immediately, and these tenuous charges dropped. Do you have any doubt regarding those instructions?'

'No doubt that they were issued, sir, but if I may…'

'You may not. Get out, and lose no time in doing it. I shall call on the alderman later today. Ensure that my orders have been carried out to the letter, and offer him my apologies for your rude and intemperate actions.'

'Very good sir,' Francis replied through gritted teeth. He then turned and stalked back outside, cursing under his breath.

'Did you miss me?' Edward asked cheerily as he threw his travelling bag down on the floor by the front door and grinned at Francis as he sat warming his feet by the fire. He caught the look on his colleague's face and took a seat. 'Bad news?'

'Do you ever feel that you could perform your duties more effectively if those who commit crimes were judged only by juries in accordance with the facts, rather than by elected officials according to their social status?'

'You obviously forget that I was ordered by the county sheriff to cease pursuing Alderman Brackenridge regarding the stolen venison,' Edward reminded him.

Francis gave a bitter laugh. 'The man clearly leads a charmed life, since earlier today I was ordered by the *town* sheriff to release the same Alderman Brackenridge from where I had been holding him for the murder of Dickon and the burning down of our house. Not even the fact that he was identified by our former neighbour Josiah Thrumpton seemed important to

Sheriff Freeman. I suppose we'll have to exert horrible pressure on Jack Putnam — if we ever find him — to admit that he either gave or sold that knife to Brackenridge. Anyway, that's about all that's happened while you've been away, so do you have something more uplifting to report? Did you manage to catch up with the young women?'

Edward smiled. 'They are all back home. But it's a long story. I'm hungry and thirsty, and I need a change of clothes. However, I can tell you now that we have another good reason for finding Jack Putnam and lighting a fire under the soles of his feet.'

Once the supper things had been cleared away, and the fire heavily banked with fresh logs, Edward held Francis, Ralph and Emma spellbound with his account of the discovery of the women in a barn in York, the unmasking of the mysterious Richard, the confrontation between Essex and Cecil, and Essex's decision to keep the whole matter secret.

Francis was outraged. 'Another example of the rich and influential getting away with murder! Well, almost murder. They were fortunate that none of those women died as the result of what was done to them.'

'I must admit,' Edward observed, 'that I was amazed at how strong they must be. A physician was called, and it was his opinion that once the women had rested fully for two days, and been given all the food that they could consume, they would be fit to travel south. But they were denied any liquor, which did nothing for their tempers, I can tell you. And on the return journey they insisted on travelling in the litters like true ladies at court, sitting back on cushions with the side flaps open, and waving regally at the country folk as we made our way south. It took us five days in all, with overnight rests for four nights at country houses in which our travellers demanded the best food and drink, and the best chambers.'

Francis chuckled. 'You can hardly begrudge them a little fun and games, after their ordeal. But what of Essex and Cecil?'

'Cecil has been allowed by Essex to continue his journey north, since it would seem that he was engaged on genuine business for his father, which of course means legitimate affairs of state. Essex has hurried back to London, taking Richard with him as his prisoner, in case he requires a witness to Cecil's wickedness. We may also expect to hear news of a visit by Her Majesty to Wollaton Hall, once the winter snows are gone.'

'What about Colonel Waldegrave, who's responsible for everything that goes on inside that castle and its tunnels?' Francis demanded. 'Does Essex intend to let him get away with confining me in that same dungeon that the women were kept in?'

Edward shook his head. 'He intends to have Waldegrave deprived of his office when the moment is appropriate. But for the time being, we must obviously tread warily where he is concerned.'

'Do you intend to get around to telling me why the search for Jack Putnam has now become more urgent?' Francis asked with a sour expression. 'Was he involved in smuggling the women into the castle rock?'

'No, but he can provide the evidence we need to prove that Jeb Tanner murdered Ellie in The Crusader.'

'What have you learned?' Francis asked eagerly.

'I should have realised he was a wrong 'un from the very start,' Ralph muttered.

'Richard proved very helpful once I threatened to leave him tied up, in order that the women might rip him limb from limb,' Edward grinned. 'Without realising what he was revealing, he explained that he shrank from seducing and drugging any more women in The Crusader after he saw Tanner in his barrel room with a dead woman whose throat had been cut. Tanner tried to engage Richard in the disposal of the body, but he declined and scurried off back to Thurland Hall, where he was lodging as part of Cecil's company. But he told me that Tanner reacted to his refusal to help with the assertion that he could enlist the services of *a man with a barrow*.'

'Putnam!' Francis yelled with delight.

Ralph shook his head and bemoaned the use to which his stolen barrow had been put. 'It explains the bloodstains, at least,' he added, 'but I've been using it ever since I got it back, and all evidence of blood has been lost.'

'That doesn't matter,' Edward consoled him, 'since we can now put all sorts of pressure on Master Putnam to tell us how Tanner enlisted his services with the barrow, which was then used to take the poor woman's body down to the Leen. While we're about it, we can also persuade Putnam to confirm that the knife that was used to kill Dickon was in the possession of Henry Brackenridge.'

'There's something else, too,' Francis grimaced as he ran his hand across his throat. 'The bastard tried to throttle me to death when I came back here after asking some awkward questions of Master Brackenridge before locking him up. If it hadn't been for Ralph, I wouldn't be here now. So when we get our hands on him, we can charge him with that as well.'

'There's an awful amount hanging on your being able to find Jack Putnam,' Ralph observed gloomily.

Edward smiled across at Francis. 'I think I can safely conclude that we shall be spending the next few days searching for him. But I have one other call on my time prior to that.

Today's Tuesday, and I must keep my regular Wednesday appointment at Wollaton.'

Edward stepped out from behind the giant oak halfway down the rose garden, and Elizabeth gave a cry of delight as she rushed down the path and threw her arms around him.

'Thank God you are back safely! I have been praying nightly for your return!'

'Yes, the Earl of Essex mentioned your concern for my welfare,' Edward smiled smugly. 'Do I get a kiss for not getting myself killed?'

'Willingly!' Elizabeth grinned as she pressed her lips to his.

When they parted, Edward looked back towards the hall. 'Let us get among the hedges without delay, lest we be seen.'

'Wise counsel,' Elizabeth agreed, 'because you are even less welcome here since you took the Earl of Essex away. It would seem that the master now regards you as a curse upon the place.'

Once they were within the shadowy confines of their usual track, and seated on the bench halfway down, Elizabeth took Edward's hand in hers and demanded a detailed account of recent events. 'Did you manage to rescue those women? And did the Earl of Essex confront Master Cecil with his infamy?'

'He did indeed, and the women have been safely returned to Nottingham.'

'A great deal of effort by worthy gentlemen for women whom many look down on,' Elizabeth observed.

'One should not judge one's fellow man or woman by the lives they lead, unless of course it is harmful to others,' said Edward gently. 'Prostitutes are useful members of our society, and in my dealings with them I have learned that they have kind hearts and generous natures. Should one of their number fall upon hard times, the others will support them and see that they are fed and housed. I have so far failed to discover any such worthy sentiment in the hearts of those who occupy positions of wealth and privilege.'

'You refer to my master?'

'No, I refer to the likes of Cecil and Essex. They appear to have their own moral standards, aimed only at preserving and advancing their own interests. For example, and to my profound disgust, Essex proposes to do nothing to expose Cecil's wickedness unless and until he can do so to his own advantage. This is in spite of the fact that the lives of five women could have hung in the balance, had we not intervened when we did.'

'From what I have observed of life within the hall, I am inclined to share your opinion of men of wealth,' Elizabeth replied. 'My master seems obsessed with the prospect of advancement at court, and clings to his almost pathetic hope that Queen Elizabeth will visit us here.'

Edward smiled and leaned in towards Elizabeth. 'Essex swore me to secrecy regarding what we discovered at York, in order that he might use it to his best advantage at court. When he saw my reluctance, he promised that upon his return to London he will persuade Her Majesty to journey here, and ensure that so far as is possible I get the credit for that.'

'Oh, that would be wonderful!' Elizabeth exclaimed as she kissed him, then blushed. 'You must think me very forward.'

'No, I think you very beautiful,' Edward gushed, 'and I thank God that I have found such favour with you. Would that it may continue.'

'Would that it might progress beyond mere kisses,' Elizabeth blushed. 'Forgive me, but I have never felt such ... well, what I mean to say is … will you please consider taking our friendship to a higher level?'

'What, here on a muddy path?' Edward joked.

Elizabeth cuffed him gently on the arm. 'Such boldness! I did not of course mean that. I would like us to approach my master with a view to allowing you to pay court to me on a more formal basis. That way, we shall not be reduced to hiding away like rats in a scullery, ever fearful of the cook's broom.'

'But your master regards me as a bad omen upon Wollaton, does he not?'

'At present, yes he does. But if Her Majesty is to visit here, and if you were given credit for it…'

'I do not know that Essex may be trusted to keep his part of the bargain,' Edward told her with a frown. 'And even then, Sir Francis may have someone else in mind for you — someone who can be of value to him, perhaps in regard to his coal extraction.'

'I would rather leave his service than be obliged to entertain the grubby attentions of one of his mechanics,' Elizabeth insisted with a shudder. 'Even a lady's maid is worthy of better than that. But he seems to value those who dig out his filthy black riches more highly than those more inclined towards owning country estates.'

'I can lay claim to neither,' said Edward, 'so even if he were to be persuaded that I am not the bringer of ill fortune to his estate, how could he consider me a worthy suitor to the lady who attends upon his daughter?'

'He is my master, not my father,' Elizabeth pointed out. 'He would merely wish to be satisfied that you are a gentleman of honour, one who will not bring the estate into disrepute by walking out with one of its servants. As for my parents, I would imagine that their main concern would be for my happiness.'

'And what does their daughter say?' Edward teased her.

Elizabeth blushed. 'We may not go to it here in the dirt for several reasons. One is the state that my attire would get into, and my need to explain it away. The second would be the risk of being observed. And the third would involve the possible disgrace of childbirth out of wedlock. But those would be my only objections.'

'You mean...?' Edward asked as his throat suddenly went dry.

'I mean what I mean,' Elizabeth smiled coyly, 'and you must take your own meaning from my words. I have been too bold already for one afternoon.'

Just then they heard a faint call in the distance.

'Beth! Your mistress is seeking you to dress her hair! Lose no time in ending your walk!'

'That was Amy — such a dear girl.' Elizabeth frowned. 'She knows that it is Wednesday, and that I had begun my walk with hopes that I might encounter you. You must leave once I am safely back inside the house. But I hope it will not always be thus. And so, for another week, remember me this way.'

She wrapped her arms around him and gave him a warm, lingering kiss.

'Have you ever considered getting married and settling down?' Edward asked Francis a few weeks later. They were standing in the common doorway between their chambers, taking a rest from packing their belongings ahead of the transfer to their rebuilt house.

Francis looked up at him with raised eyebrows and a half smile. 'I did once, but the young lady in question then transferred her affections to a man who owned a grain mill out at Colwick,' he replied. 'Since then I have managed nicely with certain arrangements that need not concern you, since I deduce from the gleam in your eyes that you may be contemplating a more lawful state.'

'You deduce correctly,' Edward replied. 'The entrancing Elizabeth Porter and I have spoken of a betrothal that wants only the approval of her master, in the accustomed way. Her parents — whom I have not yet met — will seemingly give their blessing, not that this is required, given that Elizabeth will be twenty-three on her next birthday. But it would seem that I need to ingratiate myself with Sir Francis Willoughby so that I may approach Wollaton Hall formally by way of its front door, rather than skulking through its extensive garden like a fox approaching a hen run.'

'You made a poor start there, did you not?' Francis said, laughing. 'You failed to prevent the running off of several of his deer, which is what led us to Alderman Brackenridge and the wily Jack Putnam.'

'It is worse than that,' Edward admitted glumly. 'When I succeeded in securing the support of the Earl of Essex in rescuing the missing women, he'd just arrived at Wollaton. He cut short his visit in order to learn something to the disadvantage of Robert Cecil. It seems that Sir Francis entertained hopes of prevailing upon Essex to persuade Her Majesty to visit his estate, of which opportunity I robbed him by taking Essex north after only one night.'

'But you surely do not need the approval of Sir Francis in order to press your attentions on one of his maids?'

'Elizabeth seems to think so,' said Edward, 'and we cannot hope to develop our relationship to the point of marriage while we are meeting for furtive embraces in the shrubbery. When I parted company with Essex, he promised to tempt the queen into a visit to Wollaton and give me the credit for it, but I have heard nought of that since.'

'Nor will you, I suspect,' Francis replied. 'You were of fleeting value to him, and he has likely forgotten all about you.'

Ralph appeared hesitantly from the hallway. 'Sorry to intrude upon your conversation, but Constable Draycott insists on speaking to Francis without delay. He stood to one side, and the eager young constable peered into the room.

'Begging your pardon, but we took Tom Bestall in for burglary up in Pilcher Gate. He was the last one climbing out of the window, and we grabbed him by his breeches. He wants to see you, in the hope that we'll look the other way. He reckons that this time he'll be sentenced to swing otherwise.'

'Do I look as if I have time to horse trade with a notorious thief like Bestall?' Francis demanded testily.

Draycott looked crestfallen. 'That's what I said, Bailiff, but he said to tell you that he knows where you can find a man called Putnam. Does that mean something to you?'

'Why didn't you say so immediately?' Francis yelled as he turned to Edward with a grin. 'Looks like our luck might be about to change — care to accompany me down to the Guildhall?'

16

The constable unlocked and pushed open the heavy wooden door, and Edward and Francis stepped into the cramped cell, each holding a burning torch. Tom Bestall got up unsteadily from the straw in the corner in which he'd been cowering, then sat down heavily with a cry of pain.

'The bastards beat my legs to stop me running away,' he complained. 'I don't reckon I'll be able to walk ever again.'

'That shouldn't present you with any problem,' Francis told him, 'since you get to ride in a wagon all the way up to Gallows Hill. You even get a free tot of brandy at the inn halfway there.'

'If I tell you something important, how about letting me out of here, and pretending it was all a mistake?' Bestall begged.

Francis looked sideways at Edward. 'What could possibly be that important, I wonder?'

'You're looking for Jack Putnam, aren't you?'

'We might be,' Francis replied casually, 'but Nottingham's a small place, and sooner or later we'll come across him.'

'That's just the point,' Bestall replied eagerly. 'He isn't in the town anymore, and I know where he is.'

'Then it's your duty as a law-abiding citizen to tell us, isn't it?' Francis goaded him. 'Although you *aren't* a law-abiding citizen, are you, else you wouldn't be in this cell, waiting to be hanged. On the other hand, if you can prove that you *are* a law-abiding citizen, then of course it would be wrong to keep you in here any longer.'

'Wollaton!' Bestall yelled. 'He's digging coal out of the ground at Wollaton.'

'Sir Francis Willoughby's coal diggings?' Edward asked in surprise.

Bestall nodded. 'That's right — the diggings on the other side of the village. He digs the stuff out, and then he carries it to local customers on a wagon. He's been there a week or two now.'

'And how do you come to know this?' Francis asked suspiciously.

Bestall looked furtive for a moment, before he whispered, 'He leaves some out for those who want to go up there and help themselves. I've been up there a couple of times with a cart, and we sell it to the rich people who own the houses in town. They burn it in their fireplaces.'

A short while later, the bailiffs walked back up the rickety stairs to the ground level.

'Do you believe him?' Francis asked.

Edward shrugged. 'He's right about the coal diggings. I learned from Elizabeth that Sir Francis's wealth comes from diggings somewhere in the immediate surroundings of Wollaton — probably on his own estate — and that they're burning coal in the fireplaces at Wollaton Hall. Even some of the houses here in town have begun to burn it, to judge by the fearful sooty smell that comes from their chimneys. Thurston Hall, for example.'

'Have you ever come across Jack Putnam?' Francis asked. 'Do you know what he looks like?'

Edward shook his head. 'I may know him by sight, but I couldn't connect him with a name. But you've seen him, haven't you — when he tried to choke you to death?'

'That was from behind,' Francis reminded him. 'All I did was smell him, and that's not something you'd be likely to forget, so if and when we catch him...' His thoughts drifted for a moment, then his eyes lit up. 'But Ralph knows him by sight! Ralph once employed him, remember, and it was Ralph who scared him off when he rushed out of the house and saved my life.'

They hatched a plan and agreed to propose it to Ralph when they sat down to eat dinner together.

'He's not going,' Emma insisted after Francis and Edward had finished explaining their plan. She placed a protective hand over Ralph's wrist. 'The man tried to kill Francis, and from what you're telling me he's killed before. Ralph's not as young as he was.'

'We're not asking Ralph to take him on in a fight,' Francis pointed out. 'We just need him to go up to those coal diggings in Wollaton and see if he's there. He can wear a disguise, if he prefers. In any case, we're not saying that Putnam's killed anybody — just that he's a very valuable witness to two other murders, including that of your brother.'

'He's got a point there, love,' Ralph agreed. 'We owe it to Dickon to bring to justice the man who killed him. If Jack Putnam can help us do that, then the least we can do is help these good gentlemen track him down.'

'What sort of disguise?' Emma asked doubtfully.

Francis disappeared briefly upstairs, returning with a wide-brimmed hat topped with a large feather. 'This should serve sufficiently,' he suggested. 'Ralph just trots into the pits on his horse, dressed in his best, looking for all the world like a coal customer, with this hat pulled low over his eyes. Then if he spies Putnam, he rides straight out of there and tells us. Or at least, he tells Edward.'

'And where will you be?' Emma demanded.

'Putnam knows me by sight, even if I wouldn't be able to recognise him,' Francis reminded her, 'so I have to stay hidden somewhere until it's time to rope him and bring him back into town. Edward can follow him closely, leaving me to hang back at a distance with my men.'

The following afternoon, the necessary arrangements had been put in place. A few enquiries led them to the entrance to the coal diggings on the other side of Wollaton village. While Francis and all four town constables drew their horses into a copse of trees a quarter of a mile short of the entrance, Ralph trotted ahead with Edward by his side.

Edward had never seen a coal cutting, and he gave silent thanks for the fact that he was not obliged to earn his living this way as he watched men stripped to the waist, climbing up and down ladders that were installed in pits. Each man would re-emerge with a basket on his back, which he carried to a waiting wagon, tipping its load into the back and then disappearing back down the ladder for more.

'That man with the wagon looks like he could be Jack Putnam,' Ralph whispered to Edward. 'Do you want me to go in there and make sure?'

'That's why we're here,' said Edward.

Ralph kicked his horse's side to urge him on, and walked him slowly through the entrance to the diggings, his head low and the hat pulled down over his eyes. He made one circuit of the wagon, on which a burly-looking man sat half asleep with his hands on the reins. He then guided his horse back out more swiftly and came back level with Edward. 'That's him all right,' he confirmed.

'Excellent!' Edward replied. 'Just one final task for you. Go back to where Francis is hidden with his men, and tell him that I'll keep watch on Putnam. That wagon looks nearly full, so

I'm guessing that it won't be long before it's driven out of here by the man we're after. It'll be much easier to take him out in the open, so I'll ride ahead of him and make him nervous by looking round at him all the time. If we're lucky, he won't notice Francis and his men following behind. Then when I turn and confront him, we've got him surrounded. The important thing is for Francis to hang back far enough to not get recognised. Can you remember all that?'

'I'm not stupid,' Ralph replied petulantly. 'Good luck, anyway,' he added as he trotted his mount back to the coppice, where Francis was hiding with his team of constables.

After what seemed like an eternity Edward saw, from where he was keeping a look-out behind the horse from which he had dismounted, that the men had stopped loading the wagon. Putnam gave them a cheery wave as he flicked the reins and turned the wagon towards the exit. Edward quickly remounted and walked his horse slowly past the opening in time to be a hundred yards or so ahead of where he anticipated that Putnam would be taking the wagon west, further away from the village. Then he realised his mistake in making such an assumption as he looked back and saw Putnam's wagon heading back towards Wollaton village, where he'd pass Francis and his men once he'd gone a quarter of a mile or so.

Edward cantered his horse urgently past the wagon, waving cheerily to Putnam as he overtook him. He then slowed his horse to a walking pace so as to keep barely a hundred yards ahead of the wagon as it travelled at approximately the same speed. Edward calculated that Putnam would be made nervous by his manoeuvre, and wouldn't look too closely at the coppice as he passed it. His guess proved accurate, and as Edward looked back meaningfully towards Putnam, he could see the fear in the man's face as he looked resolutely ahead. Edward decided to wait until they'd passed through Wollaton village before turning to confront him, by which time he hoped that Francis would close up behind him with his men.

Once they passed through the village, they began to skirt the high wall to their right, behind which lay the Wollaton estate that Edward knew so well from his clandestine meetings with Elizabeth. He allowed his thoughts to drift on that happy topic as he passed the northern entrance gate to Wollaton Park, then after a few moments he looked back. Putnam and his cart had disappeared from sight.

With a cry of frustration, Edward turned his horse's head and cantered back to the entrance, then looked down the main drive with its line of trees on either side. The elegant hall sat on the hill at the end of it, and Putnam's wagon was trundling slowly towards it. Francis's horse-borne team was only yards away, still on the road, and Edward came level with it for long enough to suggest a change of plan.

'Follow Putnam's wagon in there, while I enter the park through the vale gate down by the lake on the other side of the hill. I'll round up as many estate workers as I can, then come over the hill and confront Putnam. When and if he tries to make a run for it, he'll be blocked by your men, and we'll have him. That sound like a good idea?'

'It will be if it works,' Francis replied urgently, 'and it won't if you don't get down there quickly. Once Putnam reaches the house it may be more difficult to grab him, so get on with it!'

Edward kicked the horse to life and galloped him back through Wollaton village and down through the wooded area that gave access to the Willoughby estate at the foot of the lake. Once safely past the lake, he kicked the horse into another full gallop, and didn't let up until he'd reached the hut occupied by Willoughby's herd-master, Amos Blunt. He didn't dismount, but called upon Blunt 'on the authority of the county sheriff' to collect all his estate workers into a posse and assemble them at the base of the hill. Blunt looked a little puzzled but undertook to comply, and Edward rode hard to the side of the hill on which the hall was located. He then hastily dismounted and skirted the base of the hill, his heart in his mouth as he looked out over the main drive in the fervent hope that Putnam hadn't yet reached the hall itself.

He heaved a sigh of relief as he saw the wagon still at least a hundred yards short of the hall, and he smiled at the sight of Francis and his mounted constables trotting thirty yards or so behind Putnam. Then he became aware of the arrival of Blunt with the estate workers, and gave the order to move forward and intercept the man on the wagon as he led the way down the final few feet of grassy slope, and onto the drive itself.

Placing himself in the centre of the drive, Edward called, 'Jack Putnam, step down from that wagon and surrender yourself into the custody of the Sheriff's Bailiff for Nottingham!'

'You aren't him!' Putnam yelled back defiantly.

'No indeed!' Edward shouted back. 'I'm not the man you tried to throttle — he's a few yards behind you.'

Putnam looked round hurriedly, and apparently became aware of Francis and his men a few yards to the rear. He gave a yell of fear and jumped from the wagon, racing off across the lawns to his right. Edward took off after him and pulled him to the ground. They wrestled each other wildly, before Putnam was overpowered and dragged to his feet by estate workers. As he stood panting for breath, Francis raced up on his horse, dismounted, dragged Putnam's arms behind his back and fastened his wrists with stout rope. 'You don't smell any better,' he remarked with disgust, 'but where you're going, it won't make much difference. You're under arrest for attempting to murder me, and once you've had time to reflect we'll talk further about the murders of Richard Keyworth and a young woman from The Crusader called Eleanor.

'While you're about it,' Will Grantham shouted from where he stood with the other estate workers, 'you can charge him with doing me over on the night he was out here with the poachers, because I'd recognise him anywhere.'

Putnam was still struggling, screaming foul oaths and protesting the injustice of the proceedings as he was led away. Edward took the bridle of the horse that was at the head of the coal wagon and led it onto the grass. He thanked the estate workers profusely for their assistance, looked back towards the hall in case he could catch sight of Elizabeth, then remounted and followed Francis and his party as they dragged Putnam behind them on foot to make the one-hour journey back into town.

17

'I was wrong about one thing,' Francis muttered to Edward as they entered the narrow cell that contained their latest prisoner. 'He *does* make the place smell worse than it did. I think we'll leave the door open, but in case you were thinking of making a run for it, Master Putnam, I've placed two armed men in the corridor.'

'Do what you like,' Putnam muttered.

Francis gave him a sinister smile. 'That's the wonderful thing about having a man like you at my mercy — I can. For example, the last man in here was very happy to trade information for his freedom, but then he hadn't tried to kill me, like you did. Why was that?'

'I was paid to — why do you think?' Putnam growled. 'I had nothing against you personally, since we'd never met, but I was promised good money by a man who refused to pay me when he found out you were still alive.'

'The same man who employed you to steal deer from Wollaton Hall?' Edward asked.

Putnam nodded. 'No point in denying that now, since I'm up for much worse.'

'Not necessarily,' Francis told him. 'I might be prepared to overlook the attack on myself, if we just call it an assault, instead of attempted murder. If I do, it'll mean that you'll remain alive to stink the town out.'

'You want to know who paid me for both favours?' Putnam asked, and when both his gaolers nodded, he added, 'It was Henry Brackenridge.'

'You mean *Alderman* Brackenridge?' Francis asked. 'The man who would be our next mayor?'

Putnam spat on the dirt floor as he nodded. 'Yeah, *that* bastard! Was it him who peached on me?'

'No, although I wouldn't put it past him if he thought it would serve his purpose,' Francis replied. 'But while we're on the subject of that worthy gentleman, did you by any chance sell him a knife that you stole from Ralph Tolney?'

'Yeah, so what?'

'He used it to kill our servant when he tried to stop Brackenridge burning our house down.'

'Well, you can't accuse me of that, then, can you?'

'We might. But talking of items stolen from your former employer, there's still another matter that my colleague from the county would like you to clarify, then we'll leave you in peace. We might even arrange for you to be fed sometime later today.'

'What's that, then?' Putnam asked with a surly expression.

'The wheelbarrow that Master Tolney eventually got back from you,' said Edward, glaring angrily. 'It had blood on it, Putnam, and you know whose blood it was, don't you? You used the barrow to tip her body into the Leen, didn't you?'

'I like to keep things neat and tidy,' Putnam said with a grin, then stepped back as Edward lunged towards him, to be held back by Francis's restraining arm.

'You realise that you could be hanged just for helping to dispose of the body?' Edward yelled at him. 'An innocent young woman who was earning a miserable living serving ale to the likes of you!'

'There was nothing innocent about Ellie Marsh,' said Putnam. 'She'd do anything for a groat, they reckoned.'

'That's it!' Edward shouted as he turned to Francis. 'You may not want this villain hanged, but I do!'

'It was Jeb Tanner!' Putnam insisted.

Edward's face softened. 'Thank you for that, Master Putnam. We've already got Mr Tanner in a cell under the Shire Hall, awaiting presentment for the murder of Eleanor. We didn't know her second name, but thanks to you we do now. And if you are to ensure that you aren't hanged for your part in that evil business, you'd be happy to tell a jury that she was already lying in Jeb Tanner's barrel store with her throat cut when you first saw her, won't you?'

'If you say so,' Putnam agreed grudgingly.

Francis rubbed his hands. 'I think that concludes our business with Master Putnam. We'll let the Quarter Sessions decide what sentence he's to receive for his assault on me. He might even be condemned to wash. Anyway, the smell in here is making me feel quite nauseous, so let's take our leave of our prisoner, shall we?'

Edward was in the act of tying his horse to the usual tree on the Wollaton estate when he sensed movement behind him and turned in alarm. He relaxed when he saw that it was only Amos Blunt. However, the look on Amos's face was not encouraging.

'You got me in all sorts of trouble with the master,' he complained.

'Did he object to your part in securing the arrest of that man Putnam?' Edward asked. 'If so, you can have the pleasure of advising him that he was one of those involved in the poaching of the deer, assuming that you haven't already. Will Grantham recognised him, if you remember? Putnam also made a full confession when we got him into the cells.'

'It's not that,' Amos replied with a crestfallen look. 'It's because I never reported you for paying court to that Beth lass who serves Mistress Bridget.'

'You mean that Sir Francis knows about that?'

'He does now, and he was very angry about it, threatening to dismiss Beth if she saw you again. So if you know what's best for her, you'll just untie that horse and ride away.'

Edward stood there for a moment, stunned, as Blunt guiltily moved back towards his hut. 'Just give me a few minutes,' he said as he left his horse where it was tied and crept through the gardens to the scullery door. He peered round it and heaved a sigh of relief when he saw Amy bent over the sink, scrubbing out a pot. He called her name softly, and she turned, stifling a scream when she saw who it was.

'You'd better not be seen around these parts no more,' she called out hoarsely, 'else Beth will be dismissed from her position.'

'I know that — Amos told me,' Edward replied. 'Just tell Beth that I love her deeply, and that someday — somehow — I'll come back and claim her.'

'You're making me cry,' Amy complained with a catch in her voice, 'but I'll tell her.'

Thanking her profusely, Edward made his way back to the coppice where his horse was tied, then looked towards the house and gardens. One day, he'd come riding back here — perhaps at the head of a victorious army — and claim his bride, whether Sir Francis approved or not.

He turned as he heard the rustling of vegetation, anticipating the return of Amos Blunt to send him on his way. Before he'd completed the turn, he was almost bowled over by a pair of urgent arms and a barrage of kisses.

181

'Dearest Edward, just wait for me and I'll come to you! I don't care if I'm no longer a lady's maid here, if it means I can have you. I love you, and once I can leave here with a good character letter, I'll come and find you, never doubt me!'

Edward held her at arm's length, then pulled her back towards him and kissed her deeply and passionately. The tears ran down both their cheeks. 'There'll be no need for you to come to me, my sweet! One day — *soon* — I'll make it impossible for Sir Francis to dismiss me. Just trust me, and don't give your heart to anyone else, promise me?'

'My heart has been yours for some time, Edward. Since the day we met, I think. We were meant to be together, and somehow God will make it happen. I'll come to you, or you'll come to me — whichever way, it'll be God's will. Let's make a pledge now, even though there are no witnesses!'

'There's one, if you're needing one,' Amos Blunt told them shyly as he walked back into the coppice. 'But for God's sake get on with it, before someone spots you!'

'I think I may write to Essex and see if he can secure me a commission in the queen's forces in Ireland,' Edward announced as he gazed mournfully out of the sitting room window. He and Francis were now settled in their new home, and spring rain was falling on the garden in which Francis was planning on planting vegetables.

Francis looked up from the table, where the remains of breakfast were being cleared away by Molly, their new servant. 'If you continue to refuse to eat, there'll be nothing left of you to stuff into a cuirass anyway,' he commented, already weary of his companion's dreary conversation. He wished he would return to being the confident optimist who had never given up on the possibility of freeing five women from captivity.

'Then I will be killed all the more quickly, will I not?' Edward replied eagerly.

Francis had heard enough for one morning. He hammered on the heavy oak table with his fist, causing the candle holder to jump half an inch in the air, and rose to his feet. 'For God's sake, Edward! Either go out and slit your own throat, or find some doxy to divert your thoughts from she who remains at Wollaton. Do something — *anything* — to improve your humour. It's like sharing a house with one of those holy men who once roamed the countryside flogging themselves with whips! If you wish to raise your spirits, you can always attend the hanging of Jeb Tanner this morning.'

'I can take no satisfaction even from that,' Edward complained. 'He was guilty of murder, as the jury determined, and he will get what he deserves.'

'At least you have the satisfaction of having brought a murderer to justice,' Francis reminded him as he reached for his riding cloak. 'That scoundrel Brackenridge escaped with only a heavy fine for poaching deer, and although it will almost certainly ruin his chances of becoming our new mayor, we have held no-one to account for the murder of poor old Dickon.' The jury had been persuaded that Josiah Thrumpton had probably been mistaken in his identification of whoever had set fire to the bailiffs' old house.

'And that rat Putnam was allowed to plead guilty merely to an assault on you, as a reward for peaching on Brackenridge and Tanner, when by rights he should hang for the attempt on your life,' Edward grumbled. 'Little wonder, then, that I no longer wish to perform the thankless duties of a sheriff's bailiff. It has led only to a broken heart, and the ingratitude of the sheriff whose cause I served for almost a year. Even if I were of a mind to celebrate his departure from the post last week, I can summon no enthusiasm to serve his successor.'

The office of sheriff was an annual appointment, the incumbent retiring in March. Francis could rejoice in the replacement of William Freeman by Edmund Jowett, but Edward had groaned when told that the new High Sheriff of Nottinghamshire was to be none other than Sir John Holles of Thurston Hall, whose desire to impress Robert Cecil with venison for dinner had set in train the events that had left Edward nursing an aching heart.

'Even though the hanging of Tanner will take place on Gallows Hill, it's a county matter,' Francis reminded him, 'and your new employer will expect you to be leading the procession from the Shire Hall. He will not take kindly to your absence.'

'He will not take kindly to my resignation as bailiff, either,' Edward replied sourly, 'but it may as well be today. If the mob gets out of hand, I may well offer myself as the sacrificial lamb.'

Francis gave a loud tut as he threw back his cape and walked to the door, where Molly was holding his horse's bridle in anticipation of his departure. 'He wasn't always such a misery,' Francis told her. 'Some young woman holds his heart in thrall. Take my advice and steer clear of romantic involvement, since it clearly deprives one of one's wits.'

An hour later, Edward was forming the defiant words of resignation in his head as he trudged up the Mansfield Road. Behind him, Jebediah Tanner sat inside a prison cart, with his hands and feet bound and guards following behind. The procession was moving towards Gallows Hill, to the north of the town at the place where it merged into the surrounding county. A few had turned out to jeer and hurl whatever came to hand, but there was no general disturbance. Edward reflected sadly on the shortened life of the pretty young woman who'd been brave enough to advise him of the prostitutes' disappearances.

The procession halted briefly outside the Nag's Head, as tradition required, while Jeb Tanner was given the tot of brandy that was his due, in the hope that it would dull his fear of what lay ahead. Others took the opportunity to imbibe heavily in order to give them voice when the moment came.

The cart eventually halted under the gallows. Tanner was forced upright, still bound, and the noose was pulled firmly over his head and tightened for efficiency while the loose end of the rope was tied around the cross-piece of the gallows. The horse was prodded forward, Tanner remaining where he stood until the floor of the cart slid away from him. Edward watched him die bitterly.

'You must be my bailiff,' observed the nattily dressed, florid-faced gentleman at Edward's elbow.

Edward stared at him, before replying coldly, 'Not for long.'

'But long enough to accompany me to Wollaton Hall next Friday,' the man insisted.

Edward blinked. 'You are Sir John Holles?'

'I am he indeed.'

'And you are invited to Wollaton because you are the new county sheriff, and Sir Francis wishes to meet you?'

'We are already well acquainted, and good friends,' Holles told him, 'since I bought my current house from his estate. It is you that he wishes to meet.'

'We have already met,' Edward replied stiffly, 'and he cares not for me. He has banned me from his estate, so if you wish to retain his good favour, you will permit me to decline the invitation.'

'I was warned that you were a prickly individual,' said Holles, frowning, 'but you will attend Wollaton Hall with me at ten o'clock on Friday morning. You understand a simple command?'

'I do, obviously, but I do not understand why Sir Francis would demand my presence, except perhaps to curse me in the presence of my new employer. Since I came here today with the intention of tending my resignation anyway, I will deprive him of that satisfaction, at least.'

'Your resignation will not be effective unless and until I accept it,' Holles reminded him curtly, 'and I do not intend to celebrate my first few weeks in office with the need to find a new bailiff, even though my predecessor seemed to have had some reservations regarding your abilities. But in any case, the invitation to Wollaton does not come from Sir Francis, but from the Earl of Essex.'

'He has returned?'

'Not yet, it would seem. He is expected on Wednesday, and he has requested that the road from the south, as far as Hethbeth Bridge, be kept clear of sturdy beggars. Since I cannot rely on your good offices, it would seem, then I shall have to ask that the town sheriff extend his services as far south as the Leicestershire boundary. He will not be pleased, and it will hardly reflect well on either of us, since you remain in my service until I say otherwise. But be warned — should you ignore Essex's command, you will be answerable to a far higher power.'

'As I hope to be,' said Edward. 'I shall attend as required, for two very good reasons. The first is in the hope of catching sight of the woman who has captured my heart. And the second is my ambition to secure a commission in the queen's army in Ireland, which not even you could gainsay. Until Friday, then.'

18

'Thank you for nothing,' Francis muttered in Edward's direction as he strode into the house late on Wednesday evening and threw his cloak on the floor, from where Molly tactfully retrieved it and hung it on its hook. 'Thanks to your indolence, I just spent an entire day sweeping beggars out of the southern villages that rightly belong in your jurisdiction. You are still the county bailiff, as I understand from your surly utterances of late, and you should have been doing that, rather than me.'

'I shall not be occupying that office beyond Friday,' Edward replied with a grim smile. 'Saw you the Earl of Essex in the procession?'

'I saw no procession at all,' Francis replied. 'My orders were to remain a half league to the north of what, to judge by the rising dust that it created in the distance behind me, must have been a lengthy procession, with many closed litters. I was more than happy to allow the sheriff to take over my command once we crossed Hethbeth Bridge. It was he who led the procession on to Wollaton, else I would not be here now, to pick through whatever supper you have left for me.'

Francis remained in the same ill humour throughout the following day, Thursday. Edward was therefore relieved to leave the house on Friday morning to present himself at Thurland Hall. He and Sir John Holles then made the short journey west to Wollaton. Edward was apprehensive that when they were admitted through the grand front entrance to the hall, he would be recognised by Sir Francis and ordered to leave, causing more embarrassment to both himself and the sheriff. At the same time, he hoped that somehow he could contrive to at least see Elizabeth, if not actually talk with her.

Neither proved to be the case as the steward met them immediately inside the entrance hall and told them that the Earl of Essex wished to speak with Edward in the long gallery two floors up. When Holles asked if he was also required, the steward politely told him that the earl had requested only that Edward attend upon him. Grimly smiling, Edward pushed open the double doors to the long gallery and walked in.

Essex appeared from behind an arras that hid most of the extensive chamber from sight, and nodded as he saw Edward standing awkwardly just inside the doors. 'Well met, Master Mountsorrel. You have been well since our journey north?'

'Middling well in body, but sick at heart,' Edward replied. 'I take our renewed acquaintance to be a good omen for my intention to enlist in Her Majesty's army once more, this time under your command rather than that of your illustrious father.'

'And why do you seek to flee Nottingham?' Essex asked. 'Have you committed some evil act? Most men who seek military service are seeking to escape justice.'

'I seek only to escape from a broken heart, and the place wherein it was broken,' Edward told him.

Essex smiled. 'The delightful young lady who bid me watch out for your welfare the last time I was here? She has thrown you over for another?'

'No. She has been forbidden to have anything further to do with me by her employer — the pompous old fool who is your host here at Wollaton.'

'You are not the first to be thwarted in his love for a lady,' Essex told him, 'and somewhere out there in the wider world is the woman for whom you are destined.'

'There is one woman only for me,' Edward insisted. 'No other woman could inspire such loyalty and devotion in me.'

'Not even your queen?' came a voice from behind the arras, which was drawn back hastily by a page boy in rich livery who stood behind it.

Edward looked over and saw a woman dressed in a long and richly jewelled red gown, with lustrous dark red hair adorned with a diamond-encrusted diadem. He gasped, then felt a firm downward pressure on his right shoulder from Essex. He immediately sank down on one knee and lowered his head.

'You may rise,' Queen Elizabeth teased him, 'since this carpet seems none too clean. Then you may advise me why you love only one woman, foreswearing your love for your queen.'

'Forgive me, madam — Your Majesty,' Edward rasped as his throat went dry. 'I meant no disrespect. It is simply that another has captured my heart.'

'So it would seem,' Elizabeth smiled. 'She must indeed be the most captivating of women, since you apparently rescued others from a terrible fate without falling in love with them also.'

'They were kidnapped from Nottingham and taken north as hostages by a villain in the employment of Master Robert Cecil, who seems to have known nothing of it,' Essex added hastily, kicking Edward gently to signal that he was to maintain the pretence.

'And you, my Lord of Essex, displayed your customary gallantry by securing their rescue,' Elizabeth beamed. Edward was about to remind her that he had also been involved when Essex rendered that unnecessary.

'I would not have known of the peril in which they lay had it not been for Master Mountsorrel here,' he announced. 'The credit must go to him for having brought the matter to my attention, and thereafter riding alongside me as we pursued them north.'

'Indeed, and it is to my good fortune that you did,' said Elizabeth. 'It would have sullied the reputation of both my crown and my nation were it mouthed abroad that English ladies were being hawked in that moral midden that passes for a Scottish court. The nation and its people are indebted to you both. Since I have been obliged to come this far north on the insistence of our host, who also maintains that this draughty edifice was constructed in my honour, I thought it appropriate to meet the man whom Essex assures me was the real hero in all this. I have never considered Robert Devereux to be a man held back by modesty, so I must assume that he speaks the truth. And why, good sir, do you now aspire to risk your neck in my service in Ireland? It cannot be an eagerness to serve under the Earl of Essex, since I have resolutely declined to let him lead an army in my name.'

'I seek to prove to Sir Francis Willoughby that I am worthy of being allowed to pay court to she who serves as a lady's maid to his eldest daughter,' Edward explained.

'Yet you called him a "pompous old fool" in my hearing, did you not?' Elizabeth replied teasingly. 'You seek the good opinion of a pompous old fool?'

'My words were spoken in anger, Your Majesty. He has condemned us not to meet ever again because he believes me to have brought down a curse upon his estate for reasons into which we need not enter, but which were completely beyond my control.'

'And such is the depth of your despair that you seek to leave your home, abandon your honourable office and imperil your life in the hope of escaping from it?'

'Yes, Your Majesty. That sums it up admirably, if I might be so bold. Your Majesty has had a similar experience of unfulfilled love?'

Essex took a sharp breath, and Elizabeth's face grew white with what Edward took to be suppressed rage as she replied coldly, 'My only love is for my people, Master Mountsorrel. And now it might be best if you withdrew. Perhaps a turn in the garden might clear your muddled thinking.'

Mortified, Edward gave a short bow and turned to leave, then heard a rasping command from Essex.

'Do not turn your back on Her Majesty, you oaf! Bow out of the presence backwards, as even I am obliged to do.'

Feeling thoroughly humiliated, and with a deep sense of failure, Edward made his way into the gardens to the side of the hall. He was so deep in his own misery that he had not realised where his feet were taking him, until he was once again on the path that brought back such happy memories. He took a seat on the bench as tears of regret and self-pity rolled down his cheeks. His head slumped forward as a weariness overtook him, and when he came fully awake again it was almost dark.

A man stood before him, and instinctively he reached for his sword, then withdrew his hand as a familiar voice challenged him.

'Do not prove yourself to be the fool I have long thought you to be,' Sir Francis Willoughby warned him, 'for I am here on Her Majesty's command, to bring you back into the hall for a delayed supper that you almost missed.'

'I am bidden to supper?' Edward asked, mystified. 'By the man who banned me from his estate?'

'Did I not say that the command came from Her Majesty?' Willoughby replied haughtily. 'I can hardly be seen to disobey her order, since she is not only the queen, but also my guest here at Wollaton. For myself I would once have cheerfully had you horse-whipped from the grounds, but it would seem that you have somehow acquired the favour of the Earl of Essex, who in turn enjoys the favour of Her Majesty. I am therefore sent like a humble footman to invite you into supper.'

Wondering if he was dreaming, Edward followed Willoughby back into the building and up to the great hall, where supper was already underway. Essex waved to him from his seat at the top of the table, and Edward walked across the plush carpet to take the vacant seat at the very end of the top table, where he was invited to join in the festivities.

In vain he looked up and down the other tables for any sign of his beloved, then realised that it was not her place to be seated, but simply to stand behind her mistress. Edward therefore looked again down the long family table to his left, and halfway down it he saw Sir Francis's oldest daughter, Bridget. But there was no maid standing behind her, and he was just asking himself whether she might already have been banished from the house when an arm reached over his left shoulder and took hold of the wine jug in the centre of the table. His mug was being refilled as the girl serving him leaned down and whispered, 'Beth's in the room at the back of this one, and she's crying fit to bust.' He looked up into Amy's eyes and thanked her profusely, then heard a page call for silence. He looked up and realised that the queen was about to make a speech. She was looking in his direction.

'Sir Francis, our excellent host this evening, has long sought our presence here. Now that we have arrived, we are regretful that we have deprived ourselves for so long of the pleasure of being received in so gracious and luxurious a home, which would stand comparison with any noble house in the realm. Nor would we be here even now, were it not for the urgings of my trusted and beloved Robert, Earl of Essex, who had recent occasion to abide here for himself. He was able to assure me not only that Wollaton Hall is so magnificent a structure, but that it is also served by the most loyal of sheriffs, who in turn employs, as his bailiff, a gallant young man whose courage and commitment to established order within the realm is such that he was able to rescue the reputation of our beloved nation from the imminent threat of damnation in the eyes of our northern neighbour. Thank you for your hospitality, Sir Francis, and thank you for your ability to gather such men around you, one of whom I am advised will shortly become betrothed to one of your household. Is that correct?'

'It is, Your Majesty,' Sir Francis confirmed as he rose briefly from his seat, smiled across at Edward uncertainly, then sat down again.

Edward was still praying that he had not misheard when he became aware of Essex rising from his seat at the table, passing behind the backs of other diners, then leaning down to whisper in his ear.

'Never let it be said that I don't keep my promises. Now get up, because the queen wishes to speak with you. And for God's sake, either choose your words more carefully or remain silent.'

Edward rose, walked down to the centre of the table, then made the best bow of which he was capable after three mugs of wine. 'The Earl of Essex advises that you wish to speak with me, Your Majesty.'

'Only briefly,' said Elizabeth, 'and if only to prove to you that even this stern old lady knows what unfulfilled love feels like. Go through the service entrance to the left, at the back there, and claim both your rewards.'

Thanking her most profusely, Edward walked through the door and found himself in a much smaller chamber. Sheriff Holles sat at a table with a woman who had her head down, weeping. Holles looked up with a frown that failed to mask the smile he was trying to hide as he called Edward to the table.

'Should you remain in Nottingham, will you undertake to serve me, since I have not yet freed you from your oath as bailiff?'

'I will if you give me good reason,' Edward replied as he recognised the tear-stained face of the woman who was rising urgently from the table.

'Then here is that good reason,' Holles told him as his smile broadened.

Elizabeth Porter leapt from her seat and threw herself at Edward.

'I will now return to my delayed supper,' Holles announced as the happy couple embraced and cried with happiness.

A NOTE TO THE READER

Dear Reader,

Thank you for investing in this first novel in a series about Edward Mountsorrel, a sheriff's bailiff in the final years of the reign of Elizabeth I. It gave me considerable pleasure to write, since I was able to explore the history of Nottingham, the city in which I spent my first twenty-one years.

The modern city developed from two distinct ethnic groups. First came the Saxons, who opted for the cliffs that looked out over the flood plain of the River Trent. The soft sandstone proved easy to work with hand tools, and these first inhabitants were able to carve caves in which to live beneath the shadow of the parish church of St Mary's, whose own history now goes back well over a millennium. The caves and passages survived the ravages of time, and might for a while have been visited as a tourist attraction beneath what was once the basement level of one of the modern city's largest shopping malls that has itself fallen to the ravages of economic decline.

It was the invading Normans who — perhaps typically — saw the strategic military advantage of the massive rock to the west of the town as it was in the late eleventh century. They built a castle from which to defend one of the few crossings that were possible across the Trent, running almost exactly from east to west across the eastern half of England, and posing an obstacle to those travelling from south to north, or vice versa.

This rock was made of the same porous sandstone that was so easily carved through, and inevitably the castle dungeons were created underneath the main building. Further borings took these dark, forbidding tunnels down to ground level close by the River Leen, a tributary to the Trent, from which fresh water could, in those days at least, be harnessed for the brewing of beer for the castle. The brewhouse that was constructed for that purpose gave the laneway in front of it first the name the 'Rockyard', and then 'Brewhouse Yard', which name it retains today, and in which a social history museum attracts more tourists.

Those same tourists will soon become aware of another of Nottingham's medieval delights, the Ye Olde Trip to Jerusalem pub built into the foot of this rock, beloved of generations of students, and claiming to be the oldest public house in England. Whether or not it is, there has certainly been a similar establishment on that site for over nine hundred years, although its evocative current name is less than three hundred years old. Prior to that, it was known as The Pilgrim, and it took no great stretch of the imagination for me to name an earlier establishment The Crusader for the purposes of this novel, and to make literary use of the network of sandstone tunnels that wind their way down into it from the castle perched over forty metres above.

I was also able to make much use of the castle itself, for which an apology is due to anyone visiting Nottingham in the hope of finding the romance and glamour of the days of the almost certainly mythical Robin Hood. The contemporary castle is mid-nineteenth-century and sits reprovingly above the modern city, and it houses a museum. Its medieval predecessor didn't survive the English Civil War, although in its day it was a favoured residence of King John, who enjoyed the hunting that could be had in the forest to the north known as the Shire Wood, which was to become the Sherwood of legend.

Whether or not King John was challenged by Robin Hood, he most certainly was not assisted in his endeavours by the Sheriff of Nottingham, since the role did not exist until 1449, when Nottingham was granted its charter by Henry VI, and it became a borough within a county. Prior to that date, law enforcement had been in the hands of the High Sheriff of Nottinghamshire, Derbyshire and the Royal Forests. The creation of a sheriff for the town created a duality of jurisdictions that is emphasised in this novel, since the castle had been kept outside the town boundaries under the charter. The county had its sheriff, and the town had one of its own; each sheriff had a bailiff, and in this novel they were Edward Mountsorrel and Francis Barton respectively.

So who were these sheriffs, and what was their function? As revealed in the previous pages, the Shire Reeve, as the office was first described, was the monarch's local law enforcement agent and tax collector. To the sheriff fell the responsibility of maintaining the King's (or Queen's) Peace for their jurisdiction, bringing to justice those who committed crimes of all description. The worst of them would be held in custody to await the regular Assize circuits of the Royal Justices, after having been presented for trial by a local petty jury.

Such onerous duties could not be discharged single-handedly, and each sheriff would have the day-to-day work of revenue collection, court administration and law enforcement discharged under his direction by his bailiff. The bailiffs in turn could call upon constables whose work they supervised, and who were the ground troops when it came to the cracking of skulls and the application of restraints.

Enough responsibility and authority was extended to sheriffs' bailiffs to ensure that their daily working lives were full of drama, and they offer themselves effortlessly to the historical novelist. I hope that this first novel in the series lived up to your expectations, and that you are encouraged to read the remainder in the series.

I'd love to receive feedback on this novel, in the form of a review on **Amazon** or **Goodreads**. Or, of course, you can try the more personal approach on my website or my Facebook page: **DavidFieldAuthor**.

Happy reading!

David

davidfieldauthor.com

Sapere Books is an exciting new publisher of brilliant fiction and popular history.

To find out more about our latest releases and our monthly bargain books visit our website:
saperebooks.com

Printed in Great Britain
by Amazon

34016841R00116